KISMET
THREAD

HOLLY KNIGHTLEY

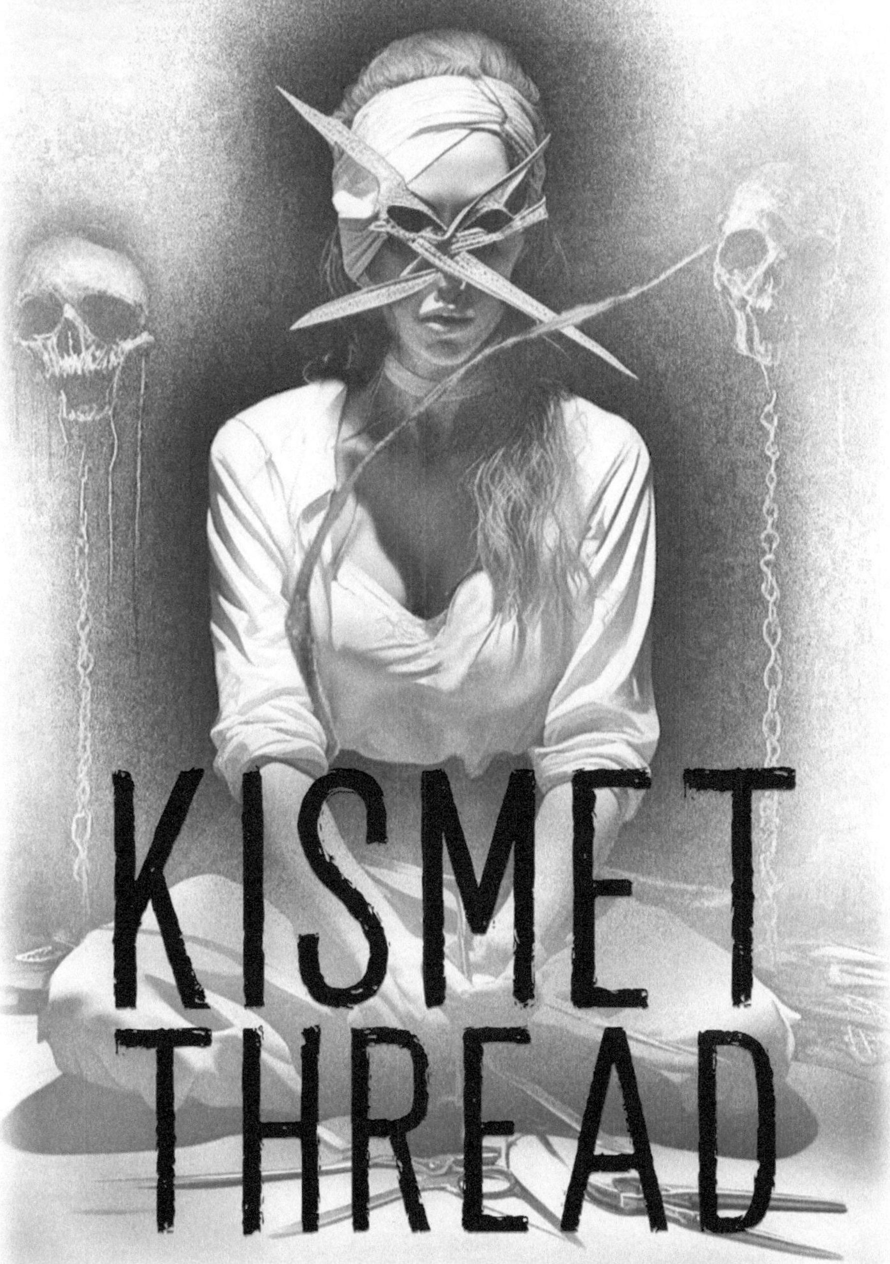

KISMET THREAD

Paperback ISBN: 978-1-958761-72-4
eBook ISBN: 978-1-958761-66-3

Cover design: AW Rabbit Designs

For Jack Cat

CONTENTS

CHAPTER ONE
Fate's a Bitch

My shovel struck something hard, forcing me to pull it from the ground to reposition it. Doing so, I took a moment to breathe. My air funneled into the cold rain like I'd just released a ghostly phantom from its earthly coil.

My breath ghost didn't stand a chance—the rain pulverized it, tearing through its airy body until it was nothing. The driving rain hammered everything. The buds from the tulip trees were knocked from their stems, but it wasn't as if it were raining flowers. That would have been romantic—like in spring, when the cherry blossoms shower the world with the pleasant scents of Easter and bright petals. No—there was nothing remotely romantic about this—these were unmature flowers, taken before their time. They would never bloom, never be beautiful, never live.

Water is the bringer of life, as the saying goes, but I couldn't believe that, not then, maybe never. The poor flowers, like the ghost I freed from my aching lungs, didn't stand a chance. They were dead and so was Jack Cat.

I moved aside a wet tangle of my hair that had snaked down the center of my forehead before I went back to digging. If I had to spend the entire day shoveling through rocks, I would. I couldn't lay Jack Cat to rest just anywhere, and my apartment complex didn't exactly have a pet cemetery. I would return Jack Cat to where we were happy, to the woods in my parents' backyard that we had played in when I was a little girl. *Ashes to ashes, dust to dust.*

This place was perfect for Jack Cat. It had a magical aura. I always thought this strange little clearing in the woods was a door to Faerie.

As a little girl, Jack Cat and I would explore the woods together, two adventurers looking for faeries. We had our work cut out for us. My backyard spanned thirteen acres, most of it covered in wild blueberry shrubs that back then came up to my waist, clinging to me with their tiny wooden teeth.

One day, our hunt led us to this little room hidden by closely rooted tulip trees. Their trunks stood tall and straight as if they were sentinels. What were they guarding? A bed of moss. A bed of the softest, greenest moss I had ever seen.

There we stood at the brink of a magical world somewhere between reality and a fantastical dreamland. I knew by the color. There, in the hidden forest cove, the green was so truly green that it looked artificial, or maybe it was just that the brilliant color made it look like it was the only thing in focus. It was as if the encircling trees were white noise.

In this hidden gem, we would wait for the faeries, knowing they had to return home soon. We would wait and while we did, we would daydream on our bed of moss as if we too were children of the woods.

Unfortunately, I had long ago awoken from that wonderful daydream that is childhood to the magicless muddle of adulthood. It was destined. Children grow up and become adults. It's just the way things are. But with me, I always felt there was more to it, more than just the facts of life. I had a destiny. If I tried to deviate from it, I'd find my way back on course as if guided by an invisible hand.

Perhaps this feeling came from being named Juliet. I was named for Shakespeare's star-crossed heroine who was fated to love and fated to die because of that love. That's how I felt—not that I was a tragic heroine, but that I was star-crossed, not just in love but in life. As soon as I inevitably woke up from my childhood, nothing, and I mean nothing, went right. Yet, at the same time, it felt like that was the way it was meant to be. As Shakespeare so elegantly put: *Some are born great.* I reason that some are born mediocre and were destined to be so. Welcome to my life.

I had wanted to go to college out of state, but only in-state colleges accepted me. I had wanted to dye my hair blonde but every time I tried, it came out clown orange and I was forced to go back to my natural color or join the circus. I wanted to be a dentist, but all I could get into was hygiene school. It was like I couldn't escape what I was born to be—mediocre, plain, and ridiculously tall.

That's the way the cookie crumbles; the fortune cookie that is. I was destined to grow up and up and up until I was taller than most men. Destined to be spit on for a living without making the big bucks. Destined to date jerks. Destined to bury my best friend in the rain before work, because I was destined to work for an asshole dentist who thought burying your beloved pet was not a good reason to call out.

I should mention I have a type. I don't blame myself, I blame fate, destiny, kismet, whatever you want to call it, it was written in the stars. I'm drawn to jerks like flies to cow patties. Whether it be friends, bosses, or lovers, I was constantly surrounded by jerks. And today my boss and boyfriend proved to be topnotch jerkweeds. I wish I could fire my boss, but that was impossible. Rick, on the other hand, I could do something about him.

"We all have to die." That's what Rick said to me when I told him, tears streaming down my face like water rapids, that Jack Cat died. He had no empathy, no sympathy. He didn't care that after seventeen years, I woke up to find Jack Cat dead. I hoped Rick was riding off into the sunset and over the human equivalent to the rainbow bridge to his watery death, but he was probably sitting on the couch playing video games.

As I threw his sneakers at him like I just yanked the pins from grenades, I told him to pack his crap and get out. I wanted him gone by the time I came home from work. I wish I had real grenades, real explosives. Something real that I could hurl at his head and make him hurt like I was.

There were the knives in the knife block in the kitchen. They were new, they were sharp. That would work. But that would be stupid. Rick wasn't worth going to jail over. I didn't stab him and the only explosion that happened in the apartment was me with my tears and screams. Rick survived my attack with a dumb look on his face, and I knew when I got home, he would be sitting on the couch with that same stupid expression that I've grown to hate.

It struck me, like a bolt of lightning to the heart, that Jack Cat died so that I would realize it was time to dump Rick. I hoped that wasn't it. I hoped that I wasn't somehow behind her sudden death. Hoped that this wasn't the work of the invisible hand, of who knows who, guiding me on my path.

The lightning bolt didn't awaken *Frankenstein's Monster* today but a different sort of creature that was full of just as much hate. I seethed for revenge. Jack Cat was old, and like Rick the Dick said, we all have to die, but I would read between the lines. I had to. I had a destiny after all, and being angry was better than being sad. Rick and Juliet were over, although I knew Rick wasn't going to make it easy for me, just as the Fae weren't making it easy to bury

Jack Cat in our special spot.

My anger gave me purpose, forcing my blood to pump faster. I would persevere. I was going to rid myself of Richard Redfield and I was going to bury Jack Cat in our special spot amongst the faeries of old as a queen of Faerie.

My spade cut into the natural green carpet as warm tears mingled with the icy drizzle on my face. I glanced back at Jack Cat who rested under a tree. Her small body was wrapped in her favorite blue fleece blanket that now served as a burial shroud. The bitter salt of reality made my stomach churn. I wished more than ever the faeries would come and take us away, although I knew it was in vain. No one was coming for us. Jack Cat was dead, and I was alone. My heart ached at knowing that this was the way it was meant to be.

My shovel struck a tree root. I readjusted and dug further from the base of the tree. Again, I was met with unyielding resistance. Taking a deep breath in, the cold air stinging my lungs, I forced my shovel down hard. The tree root didn't stand a chance. It was severed, the steel spade churning the rich soil. It was as dark as oil. No wonder the moss thrived here. Most of the soil in South Jersey was clay or sandy. This was grade-A soil.

As my shovel hit another root, I groaned. I still wasn't deep enough. These woods were notorious for foxes, raccoons, wild dogs and a whole lot of other critters that would dig up my poor girl if given the chance, and I wanted her to rest in peace. Relocating the spade head, I went in for another scoopful of rich soil and was met with resistance yet again. Standing on the glistening edge of the shovel, I put all of my weight into it. A pop sounded like a thunderclap, and with it the shovel slid into the rich soil.

With my scoop of dirt, I unearthed a large rock. "No wonder why," I muttered, pushing back loose strands of my damp hair with my inner elbow.

With the rock out of my way, my task became easier. The rain made the soil pliable, and not long after I had a deep hole. I placed Jack Cat along with her favorite toy, a crocheted pickle, into the ground and covered her with dirt and tears.

When I was done, I leaned against a tree and sobbed. I couldn't distinguish my tears from the rain. It was all the same now —water, set on destroying.

Realizing I hadn't brought something to mark Jack Cat's grave, I decided to use the large rock that had given me so much trouble as a grave marker, until I could get something proper made.

I picked up the rock, surprised by how light it was. For a rock that size, it should've been much heavier—much, much heavier. I reflected on my observation as I cathartically chipped away at the mud caked on the rock.

A lump of dark muck fell to the ground and my pulse elevated in a spike of adrenaline. I could feel it under my skin, steadily rising, as my attention homed in on the two round pits that made me see a face in the rock. At the end of the day, I was still the same little girl that believed in faeries. I saw faces in things all the time. A day hardly went by that I didn't see a face in a car or a house. I always saw the eyes first, then the rest of the face would appear. The headlights served as the eyes of cars and windows the eyes to a lucky home that had a face to be seen. I'd seen faces in rocks before, but in the woods, I usually saw a face peering back at me with gnarled eyes and a gaping mouth in the trunk of a tree. Rocks didn't have defined facial features like trees had. Their hidden faces were more in the colors they were; but this rock—this rock was different. Its eyes were deep-set holes.

Using the tip of my fingernail as a mini excavation tool, I continued to clear away the caked-on mud from the rock. This proved challenging as my elevated pulse had already reached my fingertips, making my hands tremble.

I had seen enough skulls in anatomy class to know what I was looking at. "Easy Jules, Halloween props these days are amazingly detailed," I told myself in a reassuring whisper. "But how did a prop get buried all the way out here?"

Unease crept up my spine. The skull didn't look fake. It's true, I'd seen life-like skulls at Spirit Halloween that would make you double-guess what you were looking at, but I could always tell by the teeth. My fingers exploratorily moved to where teeth would be found—if the rock indeed had teeth—and scraped at it, less delicately than before.

There was no mistaking it—I saw the pearly whites of teeth. Enamel is stronger than bone and this proved it. Two front teeth gleamed in stark white brilliance, despite having been buried under the ground. I was frantic now, clawing at the rock with both hands. Teeth, I knew. I had a certificate from New Jersey's State Board of Dentistry hanging on the wall next to Rick's *Princess Leia* poster. Prop skulls have teeth, but they don't have fillings. This was a *real* human skull.

Glancing back at the brown patch of earth Jack Cat was buried under, my sore eyes drifted over the green velveteen carpet that surrounded her—the richest and most vibrant moss I had ever seen—and I realized exactly why that was.

The harsh reality of adulthood washed over me with the rain, leaving my body shaking like a lone leaf on a tree branch—alone and cold and destined to fall like the buds of the tulip tree that lay around me in this cemetery in the woods. That's where I was: a cemetery. This special spot, guarded by wooden sentinels, that I believed faeries had danced around making the ground green with magic, was a lie. The moss under my feet was green and lush because it had something special to grow on, something to leech nutrition from. The soil was grade-A because it had grade-A fertilizer. Buried under my feet was a dead body and I was destined to find it. Fate's a bitch.

CHAPTER TWO
Poppy Rose Hoffman

The body I found was that of twelve-year-old Poppy Rose Hoffman. Poppy disappeared over forty years ago without a trace. My mother was a teen when news of Poppy Rose Hoffman's disappearance hit the headlines in the news. Poppy was the only daughter of the wealthy entrepreneur and banker Martin Hoffman. Poppy's family had tragically died in a fire, and she had gone missing. The online articles were a little blurry about what came first. There focus wasn't on the past, but on the now. On me in fact—on me finding Poppy Rose buried in my parents' backyard.

I was able to get my hands on the Hammonton Gazette, thinking a hometown paper should have the hometown dirt. Unfortunately, it wasn't much better than the generic articles online. It provided the same information and asked the same questions. 'Poppy Rose was found over an hour from her home, how did she get there?' Authorities were scratching their heads, although it was assumed she most likely hitchhiked. The articles online and in the local paper didn't seem to think it was foul play, sighting that Poppy most likely died due to exposure. It had been December when she left home, and no one could survive the inevitable drop in temperature that comes with the setting of the sun during a Jersey winter. Time had seen to it that she was lost to the woods, the leaves breaking down to soil as her body decomposed. And then the velveteen moss came, blanketing her eternal sleep. That was, until I disturbed her slumber.

In the days to follow, my parents had been swarmed by reporters and magazine bloggers, hoping for interviews and wanting a picture for their story. My mom worried the attention would lower the property value. I was a little more emotional about it—okay—a lot more. I had wanted to know the story too, but they were like a swarm of locusts. At my breaking point, after spotting a reporter roaming around in the backyard, I had shouted: "Let it be! Let the resting place that held that poor little girl be in peace." My words had rolled off my tongue, sounding very theatrical as if I was quoting a play, not that my intention was to come off lurid. My name may be Juliet, but I was no actress, and I didn't play into things for attention. My thespian monologue came from deep inside of me, where this overwhelming need to protect Poppy Rose had been burning since I found her, and it had just bubbled over. I was simply trying to relay how deeply wrong their behavior was. Gathering around my childhood home with their notepads and cameras, willing to trample over a little girl's gravesite for a headline, was disgusting. Regardless of my intent, the reporters ate it up—my 'Let it be' quote making the next round of articles. Like biblical locusts, the reporters were hungry for more and weren't going to stop until nothing was left.

This odd attachment to Poppy, because I can only describe it as odd, had to be, I thought, from literally holding her skull in my hands. When I realized what I was holding, the feeling that washed over me was like nothing I had experienced before. There was this pressurizing rush of dread and anxiety that had mingled with giddy excitement until it formed an entirely new human emotion, yet to be labeled. I couldn't help but feel special to have found her, yet cursed at the same time. Like come on, who does this kind of thing happen to? Never had I felt more like I was living my destiny. Jack Cat's death was the catalyst to so many things. She was the guiding hand in all of this. Dump Rick. Find Poppy Rose Hoffman. Get attacked by a swarm of reporters.

Finding out Poppy was only a kid when she met her fate took everything I was feeling and amplified it until it was larger than life. There was this ache in my heart. The hurt burrowed deep into my chest and ailed me every time I took a breath. I couldn't help but think there was something dark about finding her, dark and destined.

The magic that I thought was faeries was not faeries, but because of Poppy, because of her decaying corpse. I put a Band-Aid on the thought by telling myself Poppy had made the magic. She had turned the dirt to moss by *her* magic. And that magic should not be disturbed by reporters. The space was still special, and it was for me and Jack Cat, and it was for Poppy Rose and no one else.

Not long after Poppy was found, while the reporters were still buzzing around, I received a letter from Poppy's aunt, a Ms. Regina Hoffman. The handwriting was cursive and sprawling. I assumed from the way the lines wavered like a chart blotter, that Poppy's aunt was very old.

In the letter she asked me to come and visit her, any day, at any time, at my earliest convenience. Luckily, I didn't have to be so impromptu—she left a phone number at the bottom of the letter. I called and arranged a time to come to her home. I didn't really want to go, but I felt like I owed it to Poppy. In a way, I felt I was acting in her stead because she couldn't.

After about an hour's drive south, I pulled up to a beautiful oceanfront property in Cape May. This place would make a killer bed and breakfast with its bright gingerbread porch painted in an array of pink tones to match the pink siding. Ornate window pediments made each window look like it had fashionable eyebrows. This house had a delightful face, and I loved it. Wondering if I was indeed at a bed and breakfast, I scoured the front lawn looking for a sign, as I guessed what the house was called. *Castle by the Sea, Palace of the Ocean,* or something grand like that. Every seaside bed and breakfast had an over-the-top name and made sure to sell postcards so you could send one to your friends and family with the message: 'Had a blast this weekend at the *Home of the Mermaid,* wish you were here.'

I found no such sign. It looked like this whale of a house was a private residence. I checked my phone to make sure I had the right address. According to GPS, this pink castle by the sea was Regina Hoffman's home.

Leisurely, I walked around to the front of the large house, smiling at the fun shapes cut into the shrubbery. There was a mermaid and a fish that made me think of *Ariel* and *Flounder* from Disney's *The Little Mermaid.*

I walked up the front steps, porch stretching to each side of me, and knocked on the vibrant pink door. I waited for some time before it opened, and I was greeted with my name. "Juliet?"

"Um, yeah, Juliet Winslow," I said in a chipper tone. "And you must be Regina?"

She smiled at me, her thin lips struggling to pull up the corners of her mouth. As I had assumed, Regina Hoffman was beyond old. I can only imagine the color from her hair and skin had long ago abandoned her, leaving a milky white husk of a woman. Her face was a map of deep creases in paper-thin skin that gave you a glimpse of what was underneath it. Regina had been tall once and still was, despite that she was nearly doubled over her walker.

"Yes, yes. So nice to meet you, Juliet," she said, her voice coming out stronger than she looked. "Come in, come in, before the heat makes you weak," she urged, gesturing for me to enter with a flourish of her bony hand.

Regina was right, it was hot today. Spring was like that. Cold and raining one day and scorching the next. I scooted in past her, the air conditioning instantly relieving me.

With some difficulty, Regina closed the front door. I followed behind her as she slowly made her way into the sitting room. My eyes danced around the grand mansion, grateful for the delay. I had only stayed at a bed and breakfast once before, and that was for Rick's and my one-year anniversary last summer. The *Fisherman's Court* couldn't hold a candle to Regina's home.

My eyes moved from the ornate tiles under my feet to the gold chandeliers with their crystal prisms above my head. A sense of childhood wonder cascaded over me as I took in the ornate stick and ball gingerbread woodwork that festooned the entryway into the room we had just entered. There was something so storybook about it, as if I just stepped into my own fairytale. What a place.

Regina took a seat on the couch. It was an antique—I think a real one—and was upholstered in a pale pink brocade pattern. The entire room was pink, carrying on the theme from outside. The lamp shades were pink with pink fringes and the rug on the floor was a sight to be seen with its paisley pink motif. The warm coral pink of the walls brought everything together in a tidy pink package. The room was perfect. I'd name this bed and breakfast *The Pink Mermaid.*

"I love your home," I said, taking a seat on the couch with Regina. There were chairs, plenty in fact, but she'd made a gesticulation for me to sit next to her, so I complied.

"I've lived here all my life by myself. I never married. That was for my brother. The family life, that is," she told me as she poured me a cup of tea from a tea cart that was already in the room. Her hand shook so much, I was worried she would spill it. Somehow, her wrist remained strong, and she handed the teacup off to me with wobbly hands. "Not for the lack of trying you see," she said, adding a sugar cube to her tea. "Believe it or not deary, I make a much better old lady than I ever did a young one." Her lips attempted to smile. "I had to chase the boys and despite being taller than most of them, I never caught one."

I laughed and so did she. I could relate. I too was very tall for a woman. At five-eleven, I towered over the opposite sex, and nothing demasculinizes an insecure man more than a tall woman.

Rick stood six feet, four inches tall. That was the reason I gave him a chance. If I'm being honest, his height is his only good attribute. Regina wasn't kidding—it's hard to find a good man, made harder for tall women. Men like tall girls when they're supermodels sporting bikinis, but what happens when you're not model material? What happens if you're like me and are carrying around a few extra pounds? You end up with Rick, or like Regina.

I reasoned Regina was better off without a Rick in her life, a loser who refused to vacate your apartment. Rick had family, but he didn't talk to them, so there was no way I could push him off on them. I would have still tried, but being that I never met a single member of his family, it was impossible. According to Rick, he was the victim of a self-righteous brother, a crazy father, and a crusty old great aunt. I should have known to stay away from Rick when he told me he changed his name to distance himself from his family. At the time, I thought he was dramatizing for sympathy and just wanted to be called by the last name of his favorite *Resident Evil* character, *Chris Redfield*. The problem wasn't with his family, but with him.

I had made the mistake of putting both of our names on the lease. I paid for the place, but Rick's name was on there. That didn't leave me with a lot of choices that wouldn't destroy my credit. In fact, there was only one option. The lease was up in five months and until then I had to suffer with Rick the Dick as my roommate.

Regina handed me a framed photograph that had been sitting on the small table to the side of the couch. "This was my Poppy Rose," she said, her voice dropping to a whisper.

I examined the photograph closely. This was the first picture of Poppy Rose I had seen. The photo wasn't the best quality. It was from the seventies, when all photos had a blurred-out yellowness to them. It's funny how old black and white photographs were sharper than the first generations of colored ones. Despite the poor quality of the photograph, I could tell Poppy Rose had been beautiful. She had bright blue eyes and wavy blonde hair. She looked how you would imagine a mermaid should look. She would've been at home by the seashore with Regina.

"She was beautiful," I said, handing the framed photo back to Regina.

"She got that from her mother. My brother wasn't much in the looks department, but that doesn't seem to make a lick of difference for rich men," she said, flicking her beak-like nose. "He married a lovely woman, and they had three beautiful children. Poppy Rose was the only girl. I don't mean to speak ill of the dead, but Poppy Rose was the only one of my brother's children I really loved." Regina took a sip of her tea before she continued, and I wondered if she regretted admitting that out loud. "I'm sure my nephews would've grown up to be good men," she told me, gazing into her tea, "but as boys, Peter and Patrick were rascals. Ah, but Poppy Rose, she was as lovely inside as outside, just like her mother."

"And the boys, were they like their father?" I asked.

"I'm afraid so," she said with a thin smile, her eyes meeting mine. "My brother wasn't a bad man, but he was a taker. He'd take anything and everything if you let him. Even things he didn't need or want. It put his wife in an early grave, that's for sure. You can't give a man like that an inch; but Poppy Rose, she was a giver. A kind spirit. She once asked me to aid her in protecting a spider that made a web on the porch. She was afraid her brothers would see it and kill it."

I thought of the story *Charlotte's Web*. When I was little, I thought the same thing when I'd see a spider web—that the spider had to be protected. It was wrong to kill spiders just because we didn't understand them and found them scary.

"You sound like you were close," I said with a kind smile.

Regina nodded. "We were. That child was my heart and soul. I can't thank you enough Juliet, for finding my Poppy Rose." Tears glazed her eyes in a liquid layer, muting her brown irises. "After all these years, I finally know what happened to her," she said, dabbing the corners of her eyes with a white handkerchief she pulled from her pocket. "Since Poppy Rose disappeared, I have searched for her. Private investigator after private investigator turned up nothing. I clung to life year after year telling myself I couldn't die until she was laid to rest. And now that she is, each day I feel a little weaker." She plucked a single strand of white hair from the top of her head and pretended to cut it, her index and middle finger acting as a pair of scissors. "When the Fates say it's your time, it's your time, and mine is coming soon. None of us can hide from Kismet's thread. We all have to die." She let the lifeless string of stark hair fall into her lap as her hand came to rest on top of mine. It was warm and soft. "Thank you, Juliet. You've made this old lady's last wish come true."

I held back my tears, not blinking. It was such an earnest moment. The sincerest I ever had. In a soft voice, I said, "I'm glad I found her."

Regina reached behind her for a photograph that was on the console table behind the couch. She handed it to me, my hands cradling the ornate brass frame as if I was holding an infant. "This was the last photo taken of Poppy Rose," she said, her voice hitching.

Poppy Rose was in the center of three boys. Her brothers were easy to pinpoint. They, like her, had blue eyes and blond hair, but there was another boy in the picture—a boy with dark hair and dark eyes. "Who's the other boy?" I asked.

"Derrick, the gardener's son. There was a little get-together before my brother was to go on vacation with his family. It was such a wonderful day—warm for fall. I remember it like it was yesterday. This was taken about a month before the fire."

"I read about that. I'm sorry."

"Me too," she said, taking the photo from me and returning it to its place. "I still can't believe the police blamed Poppy Rose for starting the fire."

"What?!" I gasped, shocked. Every news article clearly stated that the entire Hoffman family, besides Poppy Rose, had perished in a fire, but I was still unsure how it all went down. The articles never pinpointed if she disappeared before or during the fire. But there had been nothing in any of them that implicated Poppy Rose as the cause of it.

"The fire marshal said it was arson and pointed his finger at my Poppy Rose," Regina said, a hint of distain spiking her tone. "If you'd told me one of the boys did it, I'd believe that. If you told me an enemy of my brother's did it, I'd believe that. He was in no short supply of them. I'd even believe aliens did it, but not Poppy Rose."

"What made them think she started the fire?" I asked.

"The only thing they had to go on was that she was missing. It's lazy police work," Regina told me while she shook her head. "They wanted to wrap up the case quickly because it was bad for the town. But I never let it rest. I have my own little theory, not that it did me any good."

My connection to Poppy tugged at my heart strings. "What's that?" I queried, genuinely enthralled by Poppy Rose's story.

"I have always thought Poppy Rose escaped the fire and ran. I thought it was possible she saw the arson and recognized them and was too scared to come forth."

"That would make a lot of sense," I said, putting the pieces of the past together. Poppy Rose went missing the night of the fire, and that made her more of a suspect than a victim to the local police force. That did sound like lazy police work.

I'd seen pictures of killers in my social media feed, saw how their eyes were funny. You could just tell they were off. A picture speaks a thousand words, but Poppy Rose's pictures spoke of only one word: innocence. I had looked into her blue eyes and knew that to be true. Nevertheless, the press was going to have a field day with this once they dug a little deeper.

"If Poppy Rose did know who started the fire," Regina said, her eyes wet with tears, "the secret died with her. The only justice for my dear niece was delivered by you, my sweet Juliet. Poppy Rose can rest now with her family." She blinked away tears. "I was told there was no evidence of foul play, but their findings are inconclusive as there was no soft tissue remaining. They believe it was exposure to the elements that had killed her."

I had read that. The online article in the local gazette had gotten that part right. Regina put her hand on mine again and squeezed. "I was told by the forensic pathologist that freezing is a lot like falling asleep, not unlike what happened with Romeo's Juliet."

CHAPTER THREE
An Unexpected Surprise

"Ms. Hoffman died happy," I was told by David of Davison and Son's law office over the phone. This was the first I was hearing about Regina Hoffman's death, but I wasn't surprised she died happy. A little over two weeks had passed since I met Regina at her home when she hinted at as much. She had stayed alive in hopes of finding her niece, and with Poppy Rose put to rest, she was soon for the grave.

I was saddened to hear of her passing, but I was happy for her. When I met Regina, I got the feeling she longed for death and eagerly awaited her reunion with her beloved niece.

What surprised me was what Regina's lawyer said next. "Yes, it's true she died a happy woman, and her last wish was to make you happy."

He went on to tell me that as Regina had no living relatives, she left everything to me. I wasn't getting the *Pink Mermaid* bed and breakfast. That was being sold and the money from the sale of the house was to be funneled into a yearly scholarship given in Poppy Rose's name to a bright young woman.

There was another property, located at 74 Lockhart Drive in Greenes Mills, that was bequeathed to me. That was once the official paperwork went through, and Mr. Davison assured me that it would be within the month. Not only did Regina leave me the 74 Lockhart property, but the property also came with a trust fund. "For the greens and the upkeep and maintenance of the property," Mr. Davison said, sounding like he was reading me Regina's last will and testament over the phone.

There were two stipulations that I had to sign off on before I could take possession of the property. Firstly, I could not sell the property. It was for my use and the use of my family. Secondly, money withdrawn from the trust was to be used solely for the upkeep of the property and had to be approved by Davison and Sons.

I couldn't tell Mr. Davison quickly enough that I agreed to the terms. A free house, where the property taxes are paid and the lawn is cut for the rest of my life, what more could I possibly want? I guess if I was being greedy, it would have been nice to have some money that didn't have to go to the property. Even with this incredible news, I couldn't quit my job—that is, if I wanted to eat. That's okay, everyone has a job. But thanks to Regina, I could cut down on my hours and enjoy life a little more. I was so happy, it was hard not to scream into the phone. I waited for Mr. Davison to hang up before I did just that.

"Shut up!" Rick, who was in the living room, shouted at me.

I cursed him under my breath. What a jerk. You'd think he'd ask me if I was okay, ask me if I needed help, ask me why I was screaming. No—of course not. If he did that, it would be because he cared and that had ceased a long time ago, way before we stayed at the *Fisherman's Court*. As soon as the key to my new house was in my hands, I was out of there. Rick could stay in the apartment and rot until the lease was up for all I cared.

I'd be cutting it close, but I had just enough time to drive to my new place, snoop a bit, and head to work. Tuesday was our late day at Brilliant Smiles and was my least favorite day of the week. It would be nice to start the day on a high. I was already soaring, but once I saw my future place, I knew nothing could or would bring me back to Earth. Not Rick, not my boss, and not the onslaught of spit that was waiting for me at work.

I threw on my scrubs and headed out. I didn't waste my time saying goodbye to Rick, who was preoccupied playing a video game in the living room like he owned the place.

It was a little over an hour drive to my soon-to-be new house, but it was an easy drive. It was straight up Route 206. One thing was for sure, I was going to have to find a new job. There was no way I was going to commute long distance for a job that didn't respect me. Revamping my resume just officially moved to the top of my 'things to do' list.

I smiled to myself, nervous excitement keeping a grin plastered on my face. My own place . . . In a few weeks, I would be free of Rick forever. I couldn't believe this twist of fate. I needed out of my situation and Regina gave it to me. She, indeed, had made me happy.

* * *

I parked in front of a large ornate iron gate. My smile was so wide now, it hurt. At once, I knew I inherited a historical property. The gate was huge and heavy and old. You don't see this kind of craftsmanship anymore. Today, everything is mass-produced in a factory. Every twist, every flourish of the iron, had the grace of human imperfection. Something about that made the gate seem alive, seem special. And this was the entrance to my home. I pinched myself, giggling at the pain. If I laughed any louder, someone would've carted me a way in a straitjacket. I couldn't believe my luck.

My eyes danced between the letter 'H' that adorned each

side of the gate. They were encircled in a wreath of laurel and holly. It made me feel welcomed in a way that made my chest feel warm and fuzzy. If the gate was this charming, I couldn't imagine what the house was like. My near-hysteria at inheriting such a home spread all over me, making me giddy. I was hopping in place like a rabbit eyeing a field of carrots. I hadn't felt this free since I was a little girl traversing the woods with my faithful furry sidekick.

In a daze, I went up to the gate and yanked on it. Locked. With both hands, I tugged on it, groaning in frustration. I had to get in. I didn't drive over an hour for nothing, and there was no way in hell I was waiting for the key.

I surveyed my options. The gate led into an equally intricate fence that was lined internally by a hedge of boxwoods. The boxwoods were trained over the gate arching over the entryway like *Edward Scissorhands* was the private gardener. The obstacles, as beautiful as they were, did not stop there. The hedge was lined with rosebushes that were in full bloom and scented the air like a fairytale. Shades of pink, red, and yellow shone brightly from where my face was hard-pressed to the antique gate. I was still trapped in my head, transported back in time, my ten-year-old self in full control. I was convinced the gates held back magic and if I could just get through them, I'd be in my own *Wonderland*. Visiting *Wonderland* would be even better than visiting Faerie. In Faerie you can't eat anything unless you want to stay trapped there forever. In *Wonderland*, especially my own *Wonderland*, I could eat things and grow big or small. "A little shorter," I muttered to myself. "Just a lick and that should do it."

I eyed the gate for a few moments, figuring the easiest way in was over it. Like any sensible adult, I planned my attack and went for it. The gate was almost ten feet tall but thanks to the flourishes in the design, I had plenty of places to anchor my feet. I felt like that eager rabbit as I leaped onto the hot iron bars and hoisted myself over the top. Not having the patience to climb down the other side, I jumped when I reached the halfway point. Landing hard on my feet, a spike of pain shot up my heels. I was definitely not as nimble as a rabbit.

I breathed in the roses, drank in their scent as if they were a healing balm. I had been right. There was magic here. So much magic. It was just like at my parents' house, way in the backyard, in my special spot.

The color on this side of the fence was brilliant. Like I had gone from black and white television to color TV. I wasn't a rabbit. No—I was *Alice,* and I just entered *Wonderland.* The grass under my feet was lush—too lush to be real. I stooped to pull up a few blades. As I had suspected, it was soft as silk. I felt goofy, as if I was on the brink of lunacy, but I couldn't help myself; I spun around. It was either that or scream, and I didn't want anyone to ruin my moment. I was okay. I was more than okay. I was a very happy girl.

My eyes waltzed over my property. I'd inherited thirty acres. My parents owned a lot of land; still, that didn't prepare me for this view. It seemed like so much more. Like I'd inherited an uninhabited planet. As if, as soon as I entered the gate, I left humankind in my past and my future was all green grass. As far as I could see, there were green hills framed with mature trees. I could pinpoint a few of them. One was a paper birch. I knew that from the white pealing bark. Just as I knew the red maple by its vibrant crimson leaves. I was in luck: there was a huge hemlock tree on the property. The miniature pinecone of the hemlock made perfect gifts for the faeries.

My mood dampened for a long moment, my heart dropping to my stomach. I realized Jack Cat wouldn't be there with me as we made our offering to the faeries of 74 Lockhart.

Wiping a tear, I started down a gravel path that I assumed would take me to my house, but it didn't. It just ended. I found myself inspecting a patchwork of flag stone on the ground. There was a small blemish in the grass amongst the blue gray stones, like an animal had used the locale as a toilet, but besides that, nothing about the area was remarkable. It was just grass and rock.

Impulsively, I scratched my head, as if that would make my house appear. It didn't and I didn't get it. There wasn't another path. Supposing it was possible the house was tucked behind a tree, I used my hand as a sun visor and scanned the property again. I still didn't chance a glimpse of the house and that seemed odd to me, even given the large size of the property.

A horrible feeling burned in the pit of my stomach. It twisted and twisted, nausea washing over me. It suddenly became too hot out. I wiped the sweat beading on my hairline with my inner arm. I feared the flag stones were what was left of a house that was no more. After all, Mr. Davison didn't exactly say I was bequeathed a house, rather the property at 74 Lockhart.

I called the office of Davison and Sons and was put on hold.

"David Davison speaking."

"Hi, Mr. Davison. Juliet Winslow here. We spoke this morning about Regina Hoffman's will. After our conversation, I decided to take a drive and see the property, but I, uh, I don't see a house."

"One moment, let me look in her file. It's on the top of the stack," he told me as the sound of ruffling papers echoed through my cellphone. "Let's see, 74 Lockhart Drive. Here it is. The main house was demolished fifteen years ago."

My body slumped, my shoulder sagging. I felt like a flower in a drought. It was now very, very hot out. "Oh no, why?" I sighed.

"It's coming back to me . . . How could I forget?" he said

with a strained chuckle. "There had been a fire some years before and it was knocked down due to safety concerns."

"Oh, okay," I muttered, deflated. Fate had sucker-punched me again. Kiss my ass, kismet. I didn't need a mirror to know I was pouting. My storybook home had been knocked down, and all that was left was the flagstone foundation. I inherited a property to only find out the house had been knocked down, just like I had inherited a boat-load of money that could only be used in the upkeep of the property. I could've restored the home. I could've made it lovely again. Tears burned the back of my throat. My dream house was only a dream and only ever would be. Reality was a pile of useless stones like the rest of my useless existence, there for people to walk all over and on the lucky occasion, spit on.

"While I have you on the phone Ms. Winslow, I want to let you know that I received your signature on those documents I had emailed you earlier. As soon as everything is finalized, I will be in contact."

"Perfect. Thank you, Mr. Davison," I said, hanging up before a sob broke free.

I walked back to the gate, my head bowed, my glassy eyes on the green, green grass. The brightness of it cheered me up a bit. True, there was no house, but the land was beautiful. It would always be tax-free land, and I would always be able to afford to keep *Edward Scissorhands* as the gardener. Maybe I could get a loan and have a trailer placed on the property until I could afford to build something more fitting. "Yeah, that's it," I said to myself, my spirits lifting. "And that folks, that's how you make lemonade from lemons."

I started my climb up the gate. I was over the top and heading down when I heard a man's voice come from behind me. "Need some help?"

I was startled; the street had been so quiet, almost unnaturally quiet. I lost my grip and tumbled into the stranger's arms. I was grateful for that. Without the assist, I most likely would've cracked my skull on the sidewalk like *Humpty Dumpty*, but then again, it was the stranger's voice that had distracted me into letting go of the gate in the first place. I turned around in the stranger's arms, unsure if I was going to give my thanks or a piece of my mind.

I was startled again, this time into silence, as if I was part of the sleepy street. I didn't believe in insta-love, love at first sight, or anything like that, despite my obsession with fairytales and Disney movies. I was old enough and jaded enough to know love at first sight was chemical. It's called attraction, and for some people that can lead to infatuation.

To say I was instantly attracted to the stranger with his sun-kissed skin and his wavy brown hair that fell into his gray eyes would be an understatement. It was one heck of a physical attraction that felt damn near primal. It probably had to do with the fact that he was taller than me and was in shape—like, really in shape. I imagined myself as *Cinderella* washing my laundry on his abs. Doing laundry didn't have to be a chore. It could be a new kind of foreplay. He wasn't a prince, but he did look a lot like a young *Jon Bon Jovi* and to any Jersey girl, that was better than *Prince Charming*.

I cleared my throat, coming out of my reverie with what I knew had to be a bright red blush. "Thank you."

"No problem," he said, pushing his hair off his forehead as he took a step back, giving space between us. "I always feel sorry for pretty girls who can't read."

A new wave of heat rushed to my face. Did he just call me pretty? Wait, did he just say I can't read? That's like calling me dumb. "I can read," I objected.

"Oh, can you?" he asked, pitching an eyebrow. He pointed to a 'No Trespassing' sign and said in a smug tone, "apparently not English. Maybe I should get the sign printed in Spanish or . . . what language is it that you can read?"

My face burned. He didn't have to be such a dick. In my excitement, I hadn't seen the sign to the left or the right, but now I couldn't help but see them. To be fair, it wouldn't have stopped me from climbing the gate; nonetheless, I was holding firm to the belief that ignorance made me innocent.

"Look, I don't really care," he went on to say. "As long as you delete the photos you took, we're good. Greene Mills works hard to keep a low profile. We don't need tourists flocking here and getting everyone upset. Delete the pictures in front of me and I won't have to call the police."

"Pictures?" I repeated, genuinely confused.

He sighed, running his hand through his hair. "You're not the first reporter I caught climbing over the fence this week."

"Oh, um, I'm not a reporter."

That made him take a closer look at me, his eyes narrowing on my *Love Bug* scrubs. "That's precisely what a reporter who was caught trespassing would say. Come on, delete the photos in front of me. I don't have all day." He took out his phone as if he was going to make good on his threat and call the police.

"I wasn't trespassing," I said, irritated.

His eyes continued to narrow until only a sliver of gray was visible. His lips did the same, flattening out to a thin line that cut across his otherwise handsome face.

I took on a haughty air. This guy was an asshole. Why did he care if someone jumped a fence? He should mind his own business. "I own this land," I said, feeling like a pioneer settler who had just stuck a stick in the ground to claim my piece of earth.

He swiped his phone on. "Nice try. I know the property owner and you're not her. Last chance, delete the photos or . . ." He waved his phone at me.

This guy was intense. He must have been a guard dog in his last life. I wondered if I could get in trouble for trespassing on land I didn't own yet. "Wait," I said palms up, trying to defuse the situation. "I'm not trespassing. I inherited the property from Regina Hoffman."

The man's stance softened. "You're Juliet?" he asked. I swear there was a twinge of excitement in his voice.

I was taken aback. How on Earth did he know my name? "Uh, yeah, Juliet Winslow."

Pushing his hair out of his eyes, he said, "Geez, sorry for the 9th degree. Ms. Hoffman was adamant about keeping reporters off the property, and I take my job very seriously."

"Guard dog?" slipped out of my mouth.

"Not quite," he said with a smile, sliding his phone back into his pocket. "I'm the gardener." He pointed across the street at a pickup truck with the slogan 'Trust the Greenes' painted on the side of it. It hauled a trailer with tools of the trade: a lawn mower, weed whackers, shovels, rakes, and a few things I couldn't identify. He extended his hand to me, "Harold Greene, but please call me Harry."

I shook his hand. "With a last name like Greene, I'd say you were destined to be a gardener."

"Destined to be *your* gardener," he said with a grin that gave him dimples. "That is if I just didn't earn a pink slip. I'm really sorry for acting . . . how did you put it? Like a guard dog. It's just that after Poppy Rose was found, the press has been relentless. I'm just trying to protect the family's privacy."

I could relate. I had felt the same way with the news teams

at my parents' house, and I didn't blame Harry. Actually, it was nice to know how much he cared. That's a rare quality in any employee. I wasn't sure why a reporter would want a picture of 74 Lockhart, but I liked that he was protective of Regina and would be of me. I felt my blush deepen. My face was nearly scorching. "I completely understand," I told him. "They keep trying to get a picture of where I found her."

"You're the one who found Poppy Rose?"

"Uh, yeah."

He tugged on his ear. "Mr. Davison did say that. I just didn't connect the dots right away. Wow, that uh, must have been an ordeal."

I faked a smile, not wanting to talk about it. "Well, don't worry. I promise to keep you on."

He wiped his elbow across his forehead in an exaggerated way. "You had me sweating it, Juliet."

"Hard not to in this heat," I chirped, playing into it.

The corners of his lips turned up. "Good. I've been taking care of Regina's properties since I was sixteen years old. Before me it was my father's job and before him, my grandfather's."

A sly smile bloomed across my face. "Trust the Greenes."

"And you can."

"I think so," I agreed. "Your work speaks for itself. You're one heck of a gardener."

"Thank you."

"Well, it was nice meeting you, Harry, but I better get off to work. I just stopped by to take a look. I'm disappointed to learn the house was knocked down."

"It stood condemned for nearly thirty years before it was demolished."

"That's a shame," I said with an exhalation that I felt through my entire body.

"A shame it wasn't knocked down sooner," he said in a low voice. "It should have been torn down after the fire killed the Hoffman family."

"Wait, this is where the Hoffman House was? As in Poppy Rose's house?" I asked, my pulse surging. That would explain why reporters were risking life and limb to get onto the property.

He pointed toward the ornate gate. "Yep, beyond that path was once the site of the Hoffman mansion."

"I guess it was too painful for Regina to restore it after the fire," I mused out loud.

"Maybe," Harry said, tugging on his ear again. I found it ridiculously cute. It was as if every time he thought, he resorted back to being a little boy. From the looks of it, I'd say Harold Greene—Harry—was in his late twenties. He was baby-faced, with dimples that lit up his cheeks when he smiled, but his body was undeniably that of a man. He had on one of those UV sweat-resistant T-shirts and it clung to him like a second skin. I appreciated that it left little to the imagination.

"Why did she finally knock it down?" I asked, still thinking I would've loved to restore it, even if it was the location of the Hoffman family's demise.

"My little sister died in it. After that, Ms. Hoffman had it demolished."

"Oh," I gasped caught off-guard. I could feel my face twist. "I'm sorry."

He was tugging on his ear again. "Thank you. Sorry to be so blunt. There's not a nice way to put it. Let's just say you're not the only one who ignored the 'No Trespassing' signs. Like I said, my father maintained the property. I would sneak into the house looking for ghosts. Playing chicken and hide and seek was typical."

He tucked his bangs behind his ears, giving way to an exaggerated sigh. "We were just stupid kids. The night that Stephie died, the stairs collapsed, and that was it. She was gone, and the next day the house was leveled."

"I'm so sorry," I said, not knowing what else to say.

"No one more than me. My sister was only a few steps from me when the part of the stairs she was on just crumbled under her feet. Ms. Hoffman felt sorry for my family and paid for the funeral and so much more. To be honest, I thought she would leave the property to me. I was the only one at her funeral."

"I didn't know she passed. Otherwise, I would have gone."

"I can tell that you would have. And I wish you did, so we could have met without me threatening to call the cops on you," he said with a smile.

I returned the sentiment. "Well, at least now I know how strong your work ethic is."

"There's the silver lining," he said.

"That, and Regina left funds to have the estate gardened forever. So, she did take care of you. Well, through me, she's taking care of you."

"What about the cottage?" he asked.

"Cottage?" I parroted. Mr. Davison didn't say anything about a cottage.

"The gardener's cottage. It's on the back side of the property. My great grandfather built it, but I don't own it. You do now. Ms. Hoffman let me live there rent-free as compensation for my sister, but I guess that's going to change now."

My mind went back to the morning, to what Mr. Davison said: The care of the greens and the grounds. I realized *the greens* meant Harry Greene and his family. I wondered why she just didn't leave it all to Harry. After all, the only house on the property was occupied and I couldn't boot out the tenant. I think it would've made more sense to cut me out of the equation. If anything, just give me a little money for finding Poppy Rose.

I shouldn't complain. Regina didn't have to leave me anything. It wasn't like there was no value in 74 Lockhart. Having your taxes paid for you in a state like New Jersey is a huge boon. Sometimes you have to help the miracle along. I would get my trailer and live happily ever after.

"I think Regina has it all worked out for you. I wouldn't worry," I told him. "I'll check with Mr. Davison to clarify."

"Okay, good," he said. "I've become attached to the property."

"It's a beautiful property," I said wistfully, wishing I had a house to go with the green grass.

He smiled as if it was him I had just called beautiful, but one *could* argue it was his hard work that made the property feel like you just stepped into a storybook. "Hey, uh, I was just about to go grab lunch. You want to join me? My treat. I can fill you in on other Greene Mills drama. Like the cow that caused a twenty-minute traffic jam last week."

I gestured to my scrubs. "I'd really like that, but I'll have to take a rain check."

"Of course," he said, slapping his forehead with the palm of his hand. "You said you had to go to work and here I am keeping you from it. Sorry."

"No worries."

I climbed into my Volkswagen Beetle, my body instantly sticking to the hot leather interior. Harry tapped on my window. I unrolled it. "Hey Juliet, maybe I should get your number."

"Uh, yeah," I said, rattling off my digits. I had wanted to ask for his, but was too shy. I don't know why I was being weird about it. It was work-related. I was his client, practically his boss, and he was my gardener. We *should* have each other's numbers.

"Great. I'll text you, so you have mine." My phone dinged and with that he said, "well, nice meeting you Juliet, and welcome to Greene Mills—where you can trust your neighbor."

I smiled. I had read that on the sign coming in. I liked that. I liked that a lot.

CHAPTER FOUR

Green Grass

"Well, what do you think? You moving to Greene Mills?" Harry asked me as we leaned on my car.

"I like it enough to move here if my house was more than some flagstones. I'm not big on camping."

It was true. I did like Greene Mills. I was sure that was largely due to Harry playing tour guide to me all day. When I received the call from him last night asking me if I would be up for Greene Mills Day, a hometown celebration to recognize the birth of the town, I did my best to bite back my enthusiasm. It was bad enough that I had answered on the second ring. I couldn't let him hold all the cards. Desperate didn't look cute on anyone, and certainly not me. I'd gotten the impression his call had nothing to do with the fact that I indirectly paid his bills and more with him thinking I was pretty.

Harry had been on my brain since I met him trespassing on my own property. I had been trying to come up with an excuse to text him, but when Mr. Davison handed me the key to the front gate at 74 Lockhart Drive, he informed me that he had already spoken to Mr. Greene and that he would serve as the middleman between us. If I requested anything of Harry, I was to go through him—that way Davison and Sons could distribute the appropriate funds.

What I got from my meeting with Mr. Davison was that I

was never to lay a hand on a single dollar from the trust fund, not even to pay Harry for cutting the grass. If I knew that and Harry knew that, it left me with no good reason to text him. So, when he called, my heart fluttered. It wasn't about work. This was a date under the guise of showing me around. I jumped at the invite, probably too eagerly. I should have said I needed to check my calendar or acted like my plans were up in the air, but I was never good at playing it cool.

It was a bonus Greene Mills Day was on Saturday. Rick never worked Saturdays, never worked most days, and saw me leave in my favorite neon pink romper. I looked good. He didn't say I did, but I could see him checking me out from the corner of his eye. The benefit of being tall is having long legs, and nothing shows off your legs like a romper. Skirts could look slutty on a tall girl, but a romper could be shorter than a skirt without making it look like you're trying, thus why I preferred them. It was true, my romper was way shorter than any skirt I would ever wear. That, in combination with my flawless summer tan and high ponytail that accented my best feature—my face—I was ready to turn some heads. Yep—I looked hot.

Greene Mills was in the middle of nowhere and being such, the people at the hometown celebration looked like they came from a farm. I would've fit in with blue jeans and a tank top. As it was, I stuck out like a sore thumb—a city girl in the country, and I wasn't even from the city. On the positive side, I literally turned heads—something I hadn't achieved before.

If it bothered Harry, he didn't let it show. He seemed proud to introduce me to everyone, and I mean everyone. It appeared he was the gardener to Greene Mills. It was refreshing how quaint and homey the town was. I thought I could be happy in Greene Mills. Regina almost got me there. She got me the land; hopefully got me the boy. I just needed the house.

It was late now, the moon grinning down at us from way up high. The town celebration ended at ten. As if everyone there was going to turn back into pumpkins, they rushed home and so did we.

"True, there's no house," Harry confirmed with a nod before his gaze rested at the front gate to my property. "But you have thirty acres."

"Funny you should mention that. I was thinking I could get a trailer to put on the lot."

"As long as you don't put it on the Hoffman property."

My eyes narrowed. His tone was laced with something—caution? "What do you mean? All of the property is Hoffman property. Well, was."

"Yes, technically it was," he said as he twisted a strand of hair from my ponytail between his fingers. "But it wasn't always so. The Hoffmans and the Greenes used to be business partners. In fact, it was my grandfather who gave Martin Hoffman a chance in his bank. A bank my great, great, great grandfather started when he founded the town. Martin climbed the ranks and eventually put the Greenes out. It was my grandad's fault. He was a gambler and a drinker and once you have money problems, they don't go away. Things only get worse. Honestly, my family should be thankful to Martin Hoffman and all of the Hoffmans. He bought my grandfather's share of the bank and his land and was kind enough to let him stay on as the gardener to his old estate." Harry smiled, but it seemed sad, as if it took an effort for the corners of his lips to curve up. "And from that moment on, the Greenes were the gardeners to the Hoffmans and to all of Greene Mills."

"Wow, talk about a fall from grace. From the founders of the town to the gardeners. No offense," I quickly added. "There's nothing wrong with being a gardener. Landscaping is hard work."

He was all nerves as he played with my hair and so was I. I felt like I just put my foot in my mouth.

"None taken," he said. "I imagine it was a kick in the pants for my granddad. His grandfather made this town, and he destroyed the family legacy. The Greene family was once destined for green as in money, but now we just keep the grass green for the Hoffmans. But uh, if you're serious about the trailer, make sure it's on the Greene side. It's toward the back of the property, where the gardener's cottage is. The Hoffman mansion was built after Martin Hoffman bought the land and was constructed on the property's highest elevation facing north, so that neighbors could see his house. The Greene family home faces south and faces trees."

"I was thinking I could place the trailer over the old foundation. That's the perfect spot. I like the idea of seeing the house-lined street from my home. Trees can be creepy at night. It's nice to know I have neighbors."

"Can't do that," he said, lifting his steel gray eyes to me.

"I beg to differ," I said in a haughty tone.

He released my hair and took a step away from me. I instantly regretted sounding like an evil landlord. I felt my body recoil as I was drained of my confidence.

Harry didn't notice. His eyes weren't on me but on the gate, or more likely what was beyond the gate. "The Hoffman grounds are haunted," he said in a low voice. "You can't build on the Hoffman land."

I scoffed, but it sounded more like a burp. Quickly, I tried to cover it up with words. "Haunted, please, that's . . ."

His eyes cut to me. I was silenced by the strange look in his gaze. "It's true. I wouldn't lie about a thing like that." His attention was back on the grounds, his hands wrapping around the ornate bars of the gate. "Tell me Juliet, when did you ever see grass so green?"

Never. I had only ever seen moss that color, and that was only in that special spot in my parents' backyard. "I don't think ever," I admitted.

"What would you say if I told you I don't fertilize that grass?"

"I'd say, the soil must be good."

"What if I told you I don't cut that grass?"

I could feel my face wrinkling. "Isn't there a variety of grass that doesn't need to be cut?" I couldn't recall what the name of the grass was, just that my father said there was a special kind of grass that only grew three and a half inches, so you never had to have it cut. It was always the perfect height.

"I don't cut the grass on the Hoffman side. I don't water it, I don't treat it with weed killer, and I don't fertilize it," he said with laser focus, as he continued to stare through the iron bars of the gate. "I know lawns Juliet, and there's no such thing as a perfect lawn without back-breaking work."

"What are you saying? That a ghost fertilizes the grass and then is kind enough to cut it?"

He broke his concentration to smile at me. "Now, that would be something," he chuckled. His laughter filled the airspace around us like we were trapped in a bubble. "No, I'm not saying a ghost borrows my lawn mower and cuts the grass. I just know something is different with the Hoffman side of the property, and I wanted to let you know in case it's too much for you. This is to serve as your warning." A large grin quickly spread across his face. "Not even deer traverse the Hoffman's grassy knolls."

I knew then that he was messing with me. I joined him by his side, surveying the green grass that not even the deer would munch on. In the dark, it looked like a black sea was behind the Hoffman gate. All of the property's brilliance was stolen by the night. Not even the moon brought out highlights of what I knew had been there earlier that day.

Harry spoke to me in a whisper. "My father told me the place was haunted since before I could remember. Told me to never go there. I didn't grow up in the gardener's cottage. My father refused to live on the property. We lived in the little white house at the end of the street. We were still close. So close that I saw Hoffman House from my bedroom window every night. I think my father telling me not to go there was the reason I went so often."

"It's not your fault your sister died," I told him.

He turned to me and our eyes locked. "It *is* my fault, Juliet. But I'm okay with it. My father couldn't come to terms with what happened to Stephie, but I did. I believe things happen for a reason and that she died exactly how God had intended." He flashed me a sad smile and touched his hand to his heart. "Besides, she's always with me. I just wish my father could understand."

"You guys don't get along?" I asked.

"No. Not really. He blames me for what happened with Stephie, but I'm okay with that too. If he has to blame someone, it should be me. I'm the one who brought her to Hoffman House that night."

My hand went to his arm.

"My father was wrong about the house being haunted. It's more than that. It's in the ground. Don't be fooled by its looks, it's sick, Juliet. I try to take care of it, but a sickness is a lot like money problems—once you're inflicted, things get worse. It's why I'm so vigilant about the place and why I keep it extra nice. I don't want kids to wander onto the property. And now thanks to you," he said with a playful smile, "I have to worry about reporters too."

I felt ashamed for saying I wanted to place my trailer over the house's ashes. Poppy Rose's family had perished there, and

Harry lost his little sister right before his eyes. It was a somber place and should be respected. I couldn't believe how insensitive I had been. I was sure I ruined any chance I had with him. He was already way out of my league, and now this. He probably thought I was a cold-hearted bitch.

Harry's eyes were glassy. The moonlight reflected their liquid surface. I felt like I could've got lost in those gray wells of pain forever.

Running my hand down my arms at a sudden chill, I made him a promise. "I promise not to put my trailer on the Hoffman side."

A smile teased the corners of his lips, washing away his pensive look. "Good. That, by default, would make us neighbors and since I've already shown you all the best spots in town, Matt's Seafood and The Dairy Den, I think it's fitting I show you the Greene side of the Hoffman property too."

"I agree," I said, excitement building in my core. Apparently, I didn't crush my chances. This was happening. But boy oh boy, did Harry go out of his way to find an excuse to invite me to his place.

CHAPTER FIVE
The Boy with the Match

I followed behind Harry in my *bug*. He said it was easier to drive around the block and enter the Greene side of the property from the back gate than it would be to drive through the Hoffman gate. He would know, so I hopped in my car and let him lead the way.

The ornate iron fence from the front entrance wrapped around the entire property. The same went for the boxwoods and the roses. Harry had a full-time job just with the Hoffman estate, let alone the rest of Greene Mills.

I let my car idle as Harry got out of his truck and opened a gate very similar to the one I had climbed over; the difference being the letter 'G' adorned this handmade beauty.

Once through the gate, I parked next to Harry and got out of my car, my eyes making a beeline for the gardener's cottage. It was cast in a warm amber glow by the porch lights, making the white house appear honey-colored and welcoming. It was surrounded by tall tulip trees, the same variety that had surrounded Poppy Rose. There was no wonder I hadn't seen the cottage from the other side of the property. It was completely hidden away. Hidden and exactly the kind of house I was hoping to find on the Hoffman side. It had decorative gingerbread trim and little windows that came to a steep point that looked like arched eyebrows. The house had a face. It looked wise. It was a lovely little wise house with a porch that ran the length of it like a man's mustache. The porch had four rocking chairs inviting you to sit. Large ceramic planters filled with cascading plants flanked the front door, filling the night air with sweetness. "These are beautiful," I said, my fingertips grazing a plant with small white flowers in the shape of bells.

"Thank you," Harry said, pulling his keyring from his pocket. He pointed to a building adjacent to the east side of the porch. "I grow my own flowers in the greenhouse."

"Impressive," I said, meaning it.

"Glad I impressed you," he replied with a Cheshire Cat grin before pushing open the front door.

I was disappointed with the inside of the cottage. All of the charm was left at the door. The inside was one big open concept man cave. Don't get me wrong, it was clean, as if Harry had expected me to go back to his place, but at the same time the house stunk of masculinity. There was a weight bench in the corner and a big screen television that was too large for the space. The biggest eye sore was the sleeper sofa that was already pulled out to make a bed. "Subtle," I said, pointing at it.

A rosy blush spread across the bridge of his nose. "Uh, my uh, the house was just an empty shell when I moved in. It used to be used as a storage shed. I'm not much for design unless it has to do with landscaping, so I just kinda left things how I found them. So, I don't have an official bedroom. I, uh, don't use the upstairs of the house," he said, his eyes darting to the staircase that divided the living and sleeping area from the kitchen. "It's full of stuff from the Hoffman House. Ms. Hoffman never wanted to throw it out or go through it. Now that she's gone, I guess I should. It would be nice not to have my bedroom in the living room."

He leaned against his kitchen counter. "Um, would you like a drink?"

"Sure," I said, feeling as awkward as he sounded. I hated the excruciating feeling that came with waiting for someone to make the first move.

He handed me a glass of iced tea just as a shaggy gray cat made its way into the kitchen and jumped onto the countertop. Harry picked it up and snuggled the feline to his face. The cat seemed pleased by the interaction and purred like a motorboat. "Juliet, meet Romeo."

"You're kidding?" I said, a smile warming my face.

"Nope."

"Nice to meet you, Romeo. Aren't you a beautiful boy?" I said in a cutesy tone as I petted the side of the cat's face. I was beyond delighted Harry was a cat guy. Rick never was.

"Now don't you go falling in love with my cat."

"I don't know, with a face like that, it's gonna be hard," I gushed. Romeo was a stunning cat with bright emerald eyes. His fur looked almost silver, and he had a bushy tail that reminded me of one of those fancy feather dusters.

"Well, I suppose the upside to you falling in love with my cat would be that you would have to come here to see him."

"That's true enough," I said matter-of-factly as I continued to caress Romeo between the ears. He seemed to really like me. I didn't think it was possible, but his purring intensified.

"I don't know . . ." Harry said, drawing out his words. "If I were you, I would go for the cat's owner over the cat."

"You would?" I asked, glancing up to meet his gaze as heat prickled my skin.

"Yeah, things didn't turn out so good for Romeo and Juliet but Harry and Juliet, that has a nice ring to it." He leaned in, pressing a chaste kiss to my lips, his cat still in his arms. Romeo wiggled free and jumped down. Harry put his finger in my belt loop and pulled me closer to him, deepening his kiss. I placed my glass on the counter, my hand running over the corded muscles in his back.

"All day long I've been wondering how I'm supposed to get you out of this," he said, playing with a faux button on the front of my romper."

"So, what's your plan of attack?" I asked, attempting to be cute. I wasn't the flirty type, but then again, I never found myself in a situation to be flirty. It was fun to tease him a little. With Harry I felt seen, and that made me feel sexy in a way I had never felt before. With him, I was anything but mediocre, plain, and ridiculously tall.

"I decided after The Dairy Den that I was just going to ask you nicely to undress."

"That's not very creative. I think you can do better," I teased.

A wide grin bloomed across his face. He reached his arm around my back, his hand traveling from the top of my buttocks to the nape of my neck. "There's no zipper," he whispered in my ear. "Faux buttons and no zipper . . . You must have found one hell of a *creative* way to put this thing on."

"Maybe," I said, my smile widening.

"Don't I get points for telling you exactly what I want?" he asked in a husky tone.

My smile was ear to ear now.

"No games," he said. "I want you, Juliet. I want you naked."

No man had ever said that to me before. My entire body was hot. "I'll give you a *pointer*," I whispered, my voice failing me. "My romper is spandex."

* * *

Harry was sound asleep on his stomach. His breathing almost sounded like purring. Me on the other hand, I was wide awake. I was way too excited to sleep. I had never had sex like that. I didn't think it was possible.

It wasn't surprising Harry fell asleep right away. Rick always did and he never broke a sweat. Sex with Harry was like an acrobatic circus act. Our *Cirque du Solei* performance was amazing and thrilling and downright exhilarating, but I was sure I was going to be sore tomorrow from using muscles I didn't know I had.

My eyes danced over his back to the sheet that cut across his butt cheeks. Harry didn't have a farmer's tan in the traditional way, but his buttocks didn't get a lot of sun. It was snow white and perfect. This guy was *so* out of my league. Which made the decision to stay the night or head home harder.

I had taken all the precautions in case we had sex tonight: I shaved twice, bleached my teeth, and packed an overnight bag, but the decision to stay or steal away like a thief in the night was always a gamble. Do you leave and have them miss you or do you stay and risk that they wanted you to leave? Either way, I had to pee. I sat up, scanning the floor for my romper. Thanks to the bright color, it was easily found in the dim light. It was by the stairs. My sandals were a little harder to locate, but locate them, I did. They somehow ended up kicked under the sleeper sofa.

Slipping into my romper was just as easy as slipping out of it. Clothed, I got down on my hands and knees to get my sandals from underneath the bed. When I returned to my vertical position, my eyes landed on a little boy, who could be no older than twelve. He was standing at the foot of the bed. His skin was white, the unnatural color of paper. His hair, his T-shirt and pants were all entirely black. They had an iridescent shine to them as if they were made of oil. He was solid, but his dark tangles and clothes seemed to undulate like a leaf sailing across a puddle, sending faint ripples out in all directions.

My eyes were drawn to his, where two deep-set olives stared back at me. Unlike his shimmering outfit, his eyes were dull. They were distant in a way that made me think it was impossible for them to capture light. They were dead eyes, and they penetrated through me, rooting me in place.

The boy cradled a simple match to his chest, the small blue flame seemingly bright against his dark clothing as he shielded the flickering flame with his free hand.

I felt cold, instantly cold, like I was trapped in the middle of a blizzard without a coat, yet I could feel the heat coming off the small flame as if it wasn't a flimsy match the boy held, but a torch.

As the warmth of the flame grew, so did the boy's pupils. I found myself entranced by his dark globes as they consumed the white of his eyes until they were completely black.

A chill climbed up my spine with surgical precision, making sure I felt every icy prick of my skin.

I have no concept of how long I gawked at the boy before I screamed. It felt like it was only for a few seconds, but in that short time I committed the boy to memory as if I had stared at him for hours. His crow-black eyes, beaked nose, and oil-slicked hair that curled around his temples were all tattooed to the inside of my eyelids like a permanent nightmare.

Harry shot out of bed, wrapping a sheet around his waist. I raced to him, my heart heaving in my chest. "Juliet, what is it?! Are you okay?!"

My heart pounded in my chest, my words coming out in gasps. "There was a boy with a match. His eyes went black. All black!"

Harry rubbed my back as he pressed a kiss to the side of my face. "It's ok, it's just Match," he told me in a calm voice.

"Match?" I asked, my voice hitching.

"Yeah, he's a ghost."

I pushed Harry off of me, my fear turning to anger. "I thought you said there were no ghosts! You said your father was wrong, that it was in the land!"

"Hey, take it easy," he said, wrangling me into a bear hug. "Match is a good ghost. You have nothing to fear. I didn't tell you about him, well, because I thought he was a non-issue. Most of my past girlfriends never saw him. He doesn't like to show himself. He must really like you, like I do," he said, showering me with chaste kisses.

I was too upset to acknowledge Harry admitting liking me. "Who is he and why is he here?" I asked, my eyes darting around the room, looking for the ghost boy.

"He's a friend."

"A friend?!" I said dubiously.

"Yeah, an old friend. When I was a boy, I met him in Hoffman House."

I could feel my pulse warm under my skin. "So, you did find ghosts!"

"Just Match. Stephie couldn't see him. She thought I was making him up, and I thought for a long while maybe I did. Like he was an imaginary friend or something. Over time, others saw him, and I knew he was, in fact, a ghost. Which, to be honest, made me feel a lot better. The alternative, that is me being nutso, is scarier than a ghost."

"And you're not scared of *him*?"

"No, not at all, and you shouldn't be either."

"I should go," I said, my breathing back to normal. My heart was still thudding away. It seemed likely it would be doing that for a while. It's not every day you see a ghost. I wanted to hit the road before Match reappeared. He was no *Lumiere.*

"Seriously, Juliet," Harry said in a pleading tone, "you have nothing to worry about. I owe my life to Match. The night Stephie died, he warned me that the staircase was about to give way. I didn't know at the time what he meant when he pointed down the stairs, but I followed him and then the stairs collapsed, killing her. I see him from time to time. He helps me out, guides me. Keeps me on the right path and out of trouble. He's like my conscience, I guess."

"He didn't look like *Jiminy Cricket* to me," I said, wiping the tears that had rolled down my cheeks. I hadn't noticed I was crying. In the excitement, my body had just reacted.

"No," Harry said with a laugh. "A talking cricket would be way worse than a ghost."

I chuckled. I had to agree with that. I didn't like bugs. "Sorry for the hysterics. I thought the whole haunted grounds thing was a way to get me into bed."

He grinned. "No, I was telling the truth about that."

"If not, your nose grows," I said in jest, the mention of *Jiminy Cricket* making me think of *Pinocchio*.

"Yepper, if I lie, my nose grows. It started out as cute as a button, like yours," he teased, kissing the tip of my nose.

I laughed a quick burst of giggles. "You're goofy."

He quirked an eyebrow. "I thought I was *Pinocchio*?"

Playfully, I shoved his shoulder. "You know what I mean. But I have to say, wrapped in a sheet you look more like *Hercules*."

He made a fist and placed it under his chin in a statuesque pose. "*Hercules* is good."

"Well, Herc, I should get going."

He wrapped his arms around me again. "Stay the night."

"I don't know . . ." I debated. I went from having the best night of my life to just feeling icky. Like everything just felt off.

"I want you to stay."

"I have to pee," I said bluntly, feeling a little silly for having said it out loud like that, but all of a sudden, the need to go became dire. I was grateful I didn't pee myself when I saw Match.

"Tell you what, think about it when you're in the bathroom," Harry told me as he led the way. "I'll guard the door from all ghosts and talking crickets."

* * *

Leaving the bathroom, I couldn't help but feel stupid. Harry was there, like he said he would be, waiting for me, the sheet still wrapped around his waist.

He pulled me into a hug. "Are you sure I can't convince you to spend the night?"

"I'm willing to be convinced," I told him. I didn't really want to be alone, and it was a long drive home in the dark.

He abruptly picked me up like a groom carrying a bride over the threshold of their new home. The shock of it made me gasp. I was by no means light. "I do my best convincing in bed," he intoned in such a serious voice that I laughed.

I pressed a kiss to his lips. "I have no doubt about that."

* * *

I woke up to the smell and sound of bacon sizzling.

"Good morning," Harry said with a smile as I made my way to the kitchen. "How do you take your coffee?"

I sat down at the kitchen table dumbfounded. "Black and iced, thanks." Rick, in the year and a half that we were a couple, never made me breakfast. Before that, there was Tom, and before Tom, there was Eric, none of whom ever made me breakfast. The closest a man ever came was my father, and that was with McDonald's hashbrowns during one of those buy-one-get-one deals.

"Here you go," he said, placing a mug of coffee in front of me and pressing a kiss to my forehead. "Black and iced."

I pinched myself to see if I was dreaming. Nope—I was wide awake and living a fairytale. On top of a gorgeous man making me breakfast, I slept surprisingly well for being scared out of my wits last night.

Watching the square cubes of ice melt in my coffee, my smile disappeared. It was as if I was staring into a crystal ball and glimpsing my future. This feeling I had, this perfect feeling that made my heart flutter in my chest, would soon melt. The jaded cynic that I am, told myself with screaming lungs that this was too good to be true—way too good. I wondered what was wrong with Harold Greene; he seemed *too* perfect. Life wasn't a fairytale.

"How do you like your eggs?" Harry asked, glancing back over his shoulder. His eyes looked extra bright this morning.

"Um, I'm not picky."

"Is it okay if I cook them in the bacon fat? That's how I like mine."

"Yeah, that sounds good." I couldn't recall if I ever had them that way, but I was willing to give it a try.

"Romeo loves his bacon," Harry said, giving the cat, who had jumped on the counter, a long strip of bacon. The cat clenched it between his teeth as if it were a mouse and darted out the cat door. "I think he only puts up with me for food," Harry said with a deflated sigh.

He was such a cute cat dad. "I know the feeling," I told him. "Jack Cat was a very food-motivated girl."

He flashed me a smile before focusing his attention on his cooking. I watched him at the stove, appreciating his fitted white T-shirt and basketball shorts. What was wrong with him was obvious. With looks like that, there was no way he wasn't a cheater. He must have women throw themselves on the floor in the middle of the grocery isle just so he could help them up. Asking for assistance reaching something wasn't good enough. Full-on attention was needed, rescue breaths required. I was sure *Mr. Perfect* couldn't keep it in his pants.

Harry placed a plate of scrambled eggs and bacon with a side of toast in front of me along with a fork.

"Wow, this looks and smells awesome."

He grinned. "Yeah, I'm not such a bad cook. I had lots of practice playing mom."

I took a bite of the eggs. "Wow, I like them like this."

"If you like my eggs, you should try my lasagna."

"Is that an invitation?" I asked.

"You betcha. Tonight, if you're free?"

"I better check my calendar," I said coolly.

A smile played on his lips as he took a sip of his coffee.

"So, uh, last night you said a lot of your girlfriends saw Match," I posed in a leading way. I was fishing for confirmation he was a male whore.

He shook his head. "I'm not sure what I said last night, but it was only one of them: Margaret May. May was her last name, but I always said her first and last name together. It was fun to say it like that."

"You two recently broke up?" I asked, taking a sip of my iced coffee, doing everything in my power to keep my flush off my cheeks. His face seemed to light up when he mentioned Margaret May and as silly as it was, it made me jealous.

"No, years ago," he said, before shoveling egg into his mouth.

There wasn't going to be an easy way to ask him without just coming straight out and asking, so I did. I needed to know what I was getting into. I had to protect myself from getting hurt. There could never be another Rick. "So, are you more of the casual date and screw kind of guy or serious boyfriend material kind of guy?"

A wide smile consumed his face, highlighting his dimples. I could tell he resisted tugging on his ear, settling for holding his fork instead. "Both. I only casually date and screw women I want to officially date."

"Way not to commit to a woman or an answer," I said with a grin. "You should have been a politician."

His face mirrored mine, his mouth sliding into a sideways grin. "I'm kidding. I'm serious boyfriend material. When I'm with a girl, I'm dedicated to them, and I expect the same thing. I want someone I can trust."

"Trust the Greenes," I said, quoting the slogan from his work truck.

"Absolutely, my future wife has to embody that. Ms. Hoffman always said I had an old soul, and maybe I do. I'm not looking for a good lay. I'm looking for *Mrs. Right*, the woman that's going to be the mother of my children. I'm pretty upfront with that. I want a good girl who wants a large family. In my experience, women will tell me anything to get me into bed, which is fun while it lasts; but in the end, I couldn't trust a single one of them and they all had to go. This one girl told me she didn't want to get fat." He shook his head. "Can you believe that? Children are a blessing."

Bingo. There it was, why he was single. He was delusional. Maybe even crazy. He was looking to turn back time and have a wife who stayed at home and had his babies, one after the other until she died. "Some women don't make good mothers," I said flatly. I wasn't about to swear an oath that I was willing to bear his children for a homemade Italian dinner.

"To be transparent," he said, leaning back in his chair, "I broke up with my ex about two weeks ago, because of that."

"I take it that it was a hard break up?" I asked, genuinely

curious.

"No, I was relieved when it was over. I should have known with a name like Paris France she was gonna be more trouble than she was worth."

"Really, that was her name?" I asked with a giggle. "You date any other European capitals?"

"Yep, that was her real name and no, no other capitals, but I did date a Judy Garwood. Her name always made me think of Judy Garland from the *Wizard of Oz*. She was nice, but just not right."

"And Margaret May and Paris France were also nice but just not right?" I asked, fishing for more.

"Yep. The first month with Paris was great, but then she started buying me clothes. Then she wanted me to wear my hair differently. Stuff like that. I'm not a project," he said, as if to warn me.

"Duly noted. In my experience, you can't change people."

"How about you? What are you looking for?" Harry asked, bringing a fork filled with eggs to his well-formed lips.

I laughed out loud at what I knew I was going to say. "Movie love." Before he could say anything, I quickly added, "I know it doesn't exist, but I guess I want someone I can depend on and trust too."

"And kids?" he asked as he tugged on his ear.

"I'm not opposed to children with the right man."

He smiled a toothy grin. "Good. It sounds like we're on the same page."

Maybe we were. I was looking for more than I had with Rick. And as creepy as it was for Harry to share his inner desires with me about his baby mania, he was being honest, and there was something refreshing in that.

"I think so," I said. "But, um, in the spirit of transparency, I should tell you I live with my ex-boyfriend. We broke up about a month ago and as his name is on the lease, he won't leave. So, for the next few months, I'm stuck with him as my roomie and he's making my life miserable."

"Is that who you were talking to on the phone yesterday?" he asked, putting his fork down and giving me his full attention.

"Yeah, Rick. Sorry, I didn't want to answer it when we were out, but he called me over ten times. I thought it could be an emergency. It wasn't. We received a shutoff notice for the electric. To be honest, I forgot all about it. I didn't pay it when I received the original bill thinking I'd inherited a house from Regina. It's lights out today if I don't pay it. In the past, I always did but we're not a couple anymore, so I told him he has to pay it. I mean, he should pay something. I pay the rent."

"I wholeheartedly agree," Harry said with a nod.

"I say, let the electric get shut off. I'll shower at the gym."

"Or here," he said.

"Or here," I repeated dismissively.

"I'm being serious, Juliet. If things are that bad at your place, you can stay here," Harry said, keeping his steel eyes locked on me. "I don't want to rush what we have going on here, but I don't like the idea of you being unhappy where you're at. We can always clean out the rooms upstairs so you can have your own space."

"Thanks for the offer."

"It's more than an offer," he said, getting up and going to the hook by the front door where he hung his keys last night. He took a key off his key ring and handed it to me. "If you need it, you have it."

"Paris France's key?" I asked.

"No. It's Juliet Winslow's key."

CHAPTER SIX

The Little White House

Harry said I could stay at his house while he went to cut the grass at the handful of yards that were scheduled to be cut that day, but I decided to head home, despite having packed an overnight bag. I had a strong feeling after this morning's love-making session, there was no way I wasn't spending the night tonight. Harry was making me the homemade lasagna he'd promised me at breakfast and nothing's more romantic than Italian food. I'm pretty sure it's considered an aphrodisiac. If breakfast was any indication of his skills in the kitchen, I was going to be very horny. I had work on Monday and that meant I had to run home for scrubs and a few incidentals.

I also wanted to set some ground rules and show Harry I wasn't going to just sit around and wait for him. That's how attraction turns into infatuation, and I knew I was already heading down that road.

Harry locked the gate, and I went left toward home while he went right toward town. At the last moment, I decided to take the turn that would bring me to the front of the Hoffman property. I wanted to see the grass in the daylight again. Harry's strange story about the grass and his belief that there was something off about the Hoffman side of the property held new meaning for me after seeing Match. Harry and I were either both crazy, or Match was a real-life ghost.

When I'd walked the property by myself, it felt like a magical place. My impression and Harry's belief were so far apart, I had to see the grass again, had to walk the path as I did the first day I went to 74 Lockhart.

I knew I was most likely right, and the place was magical, perhaps because Poppy Rose had lived there. It was her magic after all that had turned the moss a brilliant green at my parents'. I was positive it was his sister's death that soured the place for Harry, and I couldn't blame him. Still, it was something I needed to check out, fueled by not knowing how the little ghost boy fit into things. After all, Harry said he met Match at Hoffman House.

I had the feeling Harry wouldn't be comfortable with me walking on the grass, let alone taking the path to where the house once stood, so I reasoned it was best to do it when I knew he wasn't going to be around and seized the opportunity.

I parked in front of the Hoffman entrance and got out. With key in hand, I approached the gate. Luckily, the lock didn't put up a fight, and I was able to slip right in. Locking the gate behind me, I took the path toward the flagstone foundation. The grass seemed to stretch on in an ocean of bright green. It was so beautiful—I mean really, really gorgeous. How grass could be prettier than any exhibit at a botanical garden, I don't know, but it was. The lushness of the space, and the smell of roses as they perfumed the air, was intoxicating, like I was walking through a dream.

I felt compelled to veer off the walking path, to feel the soft grass cushion my feet like nature's own carpet. I slipped off my sandals, letting the soft blades of grass caress my feet.

I noticed two thin lines running through the grass as if a shopping cart had been pushed through it. I glanced behind me. It was odd that I couldn't see a trace of my footprints in the grass, yet these strange lines were clearly visible. I wondered if a kid rode some sort of a dirt bike through the property. If that was the case, Harry was going to be pissed.

In no time, I reached what was left of the foundation of the house. Taking a seat on a large flagstone, I assessed the property. The cool touch of the blue-gray rock felt good on the back of my legs in the morning heat. I felt at peace, more so than I had in a long time. There was no sickness here. No evil. How could there be? Even with all the death the Hoffman property saw, it breathed life.

My toes nestled into the soft grass at my feet and my mind wandered to Poppy Rose again, and how I found her under a bed of vibrant emerald moss. If it was her death that made the moss green, perhaps it was the Hoffman family's and Stephie Greene's deaths that did the same here. They fed the grass with their blood. It was a morbid thought, and I wasn't sure what that said about me as a person, but did things indeed grow better if watered with blood?

I came to notice a name crudely carved on the flagstone I was sitting on. It looked like it was done with the tip of a knife or the edge of a sharp rock. The letters were faint—so faint that I wasn't surprised I hadn't noticed it the first time I saw the flagstone foundation. I could just make out 'Patrick' scraped into the stone. Curiosity tickled the back of my skull. Upon further inspection, I observed that all of the rocks had names carved into them, some names more legible than others. It looked like Harry didn't keep as many kids off the property as he thought.

I searched the flagstone for Match's name, which was pointless. There was no way that was his real name, but I checked for it anyway. I wondered if he was like Harry's sister and had sneaked onto the property and died and was now left haunting the place. It wasn't out of the ordinary for family members to set up roadside memorials for lost loved ones and I thought it was possible someone could have carved out Match's name in the place he died, but without knowing his real name, it was impossible to tell graffiti from memorial.

Harry said not to worry about Match, and I supposed there could be such a thing as a friendly ghost. Hollywood seemed to think so, there was *Casper*, but Hollywood also thought there were a lot of unfriendly ghosts too. The kind that possess you and make you projectile vomit. The only thing worse than spit is projectile vomit.

As what was expected, 'Match' wasn't amongst the names on

the flagstone. I slid my sandals back on and scanned the green foliage for a trace of the darkness Harry hinted at, realizing that I most likely had met it last night. With black eyes like that, Match had to be evil, or darn close to it. I hoped beyond hope the Hoffman property had only one ghost and that I would never see him again. The dead shouldn't mix with the living—friendly ghost or poltergeist. I was gonna sage that little bugger right out of existence. Thank you *Intro to Botany.* I knew that elective would come in handy one day.

* * *

I locked the gate behind me, tugging on the bars to make sure the gate stayed closed. Approaching my car, my eyes scanned the house-lined street that seemed to act as another fence around the Hoffman property. I wondered what house Harry grew up in.

There was a white house, but it was all the way down the row of homes. I couldn't imagine Harry was able to see the Hoffman House from there, but then again, maybe Hoffman House had been very tall—one of those three-story monstrosities millionaires seem to be fond of. I was just about to get in my *bug* when I noticed a white house on the other end of the row of homes, not far from where I parked.

The little white house was for sale. The lawn was well-kept like most of the homes on the street, but its neighbor's house was so overgrown with tall grass and climbing vines that it got lost amidst the chaos.

I crossed the street toward the house. "This has to be it," I muttered to myself as I stood on the front porch and looked toward the Hoffman property. The porch had a front row seat to the gate as I imagined all the rooms facing the street did. There was no wonder why Harry was tempted to go there. The property taunted him.

As I stepped off the porch, I heard a low-grade creak come from behind me. I turned around, surprised to see the front door of the house was slightly ajar. I surveyed my surroundings. I was alone, the street was quiet. I took the three porch steps to the front

59

door and peeked in. The house seemed to be completely furnished. "Hello?" I called.

No one answered. The door must have popped open. Old doors do things like that. I recalled my grandmother always having a problem with that at her house, something about the door swelling and the lock not catching right.

Since the door was open, I decided to look around. I was curious to see how Harry grew up. Your childhood bedroom is a lot like looking in your medicine cabinet. It tells a lot about you.

I flipped the light by the door. Nothing. The electricity was shut off. That didn't stop me. There was enough sunlight filtering in through the windows. I entered the room I thought must have been Harry's, as it was the only bedroom facing the Hoffman property. It was a generic room that had no personality. The room was painted blue and had blue accents, including the comforters on the bunkbed. Besides the bunkbed and floor lamp, the room was empty. So much for learning something about him. It was then I gathered that the house must have been staged in hopes of a quick sale and nothing I saw actually belonged to Harry and his family.

I went to leave when I noticed a wood sign hanging from a door down the hall. 'Stephanie's room' was painted in pink shades and doused in silver glitter. It looked homemade and I wondered if this could be a relic from Harry's childhood. After all, Stephie was a nickname for Stephanie.

I let myself in. The room was painted pastel pink and had a ballerina border that framed the top of the room. The bed was made and adorned with stuffed animals. The vanity was covered in cosmetics—the kind little girls get for Christmas—with colors that are so bright they make you squint. There were several foam heads topped with blonde wigs of varying lengths on the vanity. One was even wearing a tiara.

This room was clearly not staged like the rest of the home. I had a gut-wrenching feeling I was indeed in Stephie Greene's bedroom, and this was exactly how it looked when she was alive. It made me depressed to see her little ballerina dress hanging on the back of her door. She had liked to play dress up. So had I, when I was a kid. Poor Stephie; judging by the size of the tutu, she couldn't have been more than ten when she died.

I thought it was more than possible that when Harry and his father moved, they just couldn't bring themselves to clean out Stephanie's bedroom. This room had become a memorial to her. To the little girl that they missed.

I felt like I had invaded Harry's privacy, snooping around his childhood home as I did. It made me feel dirty. I'd outstayed my welcome. It was time to leave.

* * *

"You won't find what you're looking for in there," I heard as I came out the front door. My head jerked to see an old woman sitting on the porch next door. She was almost completely hidden by the overgrowth of her front yard. The summer had turned tall lumps of grass into brown husks and Virginia creeper climbed over dogwood trees, cascading the yard in shadows. Her yard had to be the only one in town who Harry didn't cut.

"H-hi," I spluttered, wondering if she had seen me go in.

She pointed toward the Hoffman property. "And you won't find what you're looking for over there either."

"Um . . ." I hesitated.

"Stay away from that boy," she told me in a steady voice.

"Uh, Harry?" I asked, raising a skeptical brow.

"I saw him, you know. I saw him carry his sister into the house that night. And I saw him return home with her blood on his hands."

I was quite speechless.

"Something's not right with that Hoffman boy."

I smiled politely. The old woman was clearly not right in the head. Harry wasn't a Hoffman; he was a Greene. The Hoffman boys all died.

"Have a nice day," I chirped, before quickly making my way across the street to my car. There was no wonder that house was still for sale—with a neighbor like that it would never sell.

"I see him!" the woman called after me. "I see him bring them in there, and they never come out. Something's not right with those Hoffman boys—the both of them! I saw the blood on both of their hands.!"

"Peter and Patrick are dead," I muttered under my breath as I got into my car.

CHAPTER SEVEN

A Push in the Right Direction

"The electricity's been shut off," Rick hissed at me as soon as I opened the door to my apartment.

"You better pay it then," I said smugly.

He hopped off the couch and stalked toward me. Grabbing me by my shoulders, he pinned me against the wall. I was taken aback. Rick had never been physical with me, but then again, I had always done what he said when he said it.

"Pay it now," he said in a slow, methodical tone.

I stared into his gunmetal gray eyes. I knew he gamed on the weekends with his friends online, but I didn't care. I told him I wasn't paying it, and I meant it. "No."

Rick slammed me into the wall, his strength frightening me. The back of my head struck the drywall with an ugly thud. The framed picture fell off the wall, striking me directly on the top of my head. I felt the burn and knew it had cut me.

He pushed his phone into my hand. "Call now and pay it, Juliet. I'm not messing around with you."

A shiver ran down my spine as I felt blood trickle down my forehead. I could handle most things with grace, but blood was not one of them. I hated blood. I guess there *was* something worse than projectile vomit. How could I have forgotten? Every time I had a patient spit out a mouthful of it, I felt nauseous. The only thing worse than other people's blood was my own.

Before I could respond, Rick slammed me into the wall again, this time harder. My blood continued its descent, snaking down my nose, the metallic smell of it thick in my nostrils. I could feel it making its way to my mouth. My entire body shook; I didn't want it to touch my lips. I didn't want to taste it.

"Okay," I said, my voice trembling.

He took my purse from me. Finding my wallet, he held up my credit card so I could make the payment. When it was done, he went back to the couch, and I ran to the guest room and locked the door. I called my mother, but she didn't answer, so I called Harry.

* * *

My phone dinged. It was Harry letting me know he'd made it to the apartment.

I unlocked the guest room and hurriedly went to the front door.

"Are you okay?" Harry asked in a rushed voice as soon as he saw me.

Seeing him, heat raced to my face, fresh tears climbing their way up my throat. "The cut on my scalp is small, it just bled a lot. Sorry I called you. I know you're busy. I, uh, just overreacted."

"Nonsense," he said. "I'm glad you called me." Gently, Harry examined the cut on the top of my head, being mindful not to touch it as he moved my hair aside. "I brought the trailer. Let's pack up everything that's yours. You're not staying here another night."

I nodded.

"Where is he now?"

"The bedroom," I said, pointing down the hall.

As if on cue, Rick emerged from the bedroom with a sour

look on his face. Harry grabbed him by the shoulders, pushing him against the same wall Rick had pinned me to. "If you touch her again, I will kill you," Harry said in a firm voice.

"What the fuck is going on?" Rick asked, his eyes darting to me.

"Look at me when I'm talking to you," Harry told Rick.

Rick was taller than Harry by about two inches, but there wasn't an ounce of muscle on him. Harry could break Rick in half like a twig.

"Easy broski," Rick said, his voice wavering. "This is *my* house. You can't just come in here and push me around."

Harry did just that, slamming Rick against the wall with so much force, I thought he was going to go through it. It was nice to see Rick suffer the way I had, to feel scared.

"Listen closely Rick, because I am only going to warn you once," Harry said through clenched teeth. "There will be no second chances with me. If you so much as look at Juliet again, I will make it so you disappear. Do we understand each other?"

"I didn't mean for her to cut her head."

Harry shoved Rick against the wall for the third time and this time, his head struck it hard, the sound reverberating in the small apartment. "Do we understand each other?" Harry repeated, not giving Rich an inch.

Rick cowered, bowing his head. "Yes," he muttered. His voice sounded small, as if it had come from a mouse.

"Juliet is going to pack up her things. I don't want you here. Go take a walk and come back in a few hours."

CHAPTER EIGHT

Upstairs

"Why do you keep it locked?" I asked Harry as I waited behind him on the stairs. After a week of my stuff cluttering his place, I decided to take him up on his offer and clean out the upstairs of the gardener's cottage. I had stubbed my toe on his weight set for the last time. Before my poor feet were permanently disfigured, it was time to find a new home for Harry's weights.

"It's locked to protect Ms. Hoffman's things from the hundreds of nosey women I bring home," he teased, pulling me in for a kiss.

"Here I was thinking I was special," I said flatly.

He pressed me against the stair rail and deepened his kiss. "You are. I knew it since the first moment I saw you."

The butterflies in my stomach rapturously fluttered. Harry did something to me. There was no denying that. We were still in the honeymoon period of our relationship but the way he made me feel was better than a drug, and just as dangerous. I was addicted to him. I would never admit this to Harry or anyone else, but I was way past infatuation. He was my air and every time I breathed him in, I felt a high that fed this sickness that was growing inside of me.

I didn't care—like any addict, I needed my high more than

anything. The sickness wasn't in the Hoffman property—it was in Harold Greene. He was making me lovesick. As his lips locked with mine and we breathed the same air, it was hard to think he was anything but *Mr. Right.*

This—what I had with Harry—felt destined, like everything I had been through had been to bring me to him: Jack Cat dying, finding Poppy Rose, meeting Regina Hoffman, and Rick being a dick for the second time.

I felt it, deep in my heart, that Jack Cat had set me on the right path. Her parting was her last gift to me. She knew it would finally bring me the happiness I was looking for. I felt batshit crazy every time I thought about it, but the truth remained the same: I was destined to meet Harry. My life was full of too many strange occurrences for it to be anything but fate.

With mock enthusiasm, playing down my true feelings for him, I said, "Oh really? So threatening to call the cops on me was because I was special?"

"You're never going to let that go, are you?" he asked, a playful smile teasing his lips.

"Nope. Never," I said as I pushed the door to the upstairs open.

Harry whispered in my ear, "I'm up for just shutting the door and spending the day in bed."

I felt the same way. We were met head-on by boxes. They were everywhere, stacked nearly to the ceiling. We had our work cut out for us, but on the plus side, the upstairs had loads of potential. Unlike the downstairs, this space hadn't been gutted and was packed with just as much charm as boxes. I loved the original mahogany doors with their ornate brass knobs that matched the brass chandeliers. There was fancy trim and crown molding everywhere. Once we got everything sorted through, I knew the space would be perfect. It was precisely what I wanted.

My nose wrinkled at the smell of smoke. All of the boxes smelled of it—stale smoke.

Harry kissed the tip of my nose before he told me, "it's from the fire. You can never get the smell of smoke out."

"This stuff is from Poppy Rose's house? I thought it was Regina's?"

"Regina's by default," he said. "After the fire, the family's belongings were put in here."

"Did any of Poppy Rose's things survive the fire?"

"I'm not sure." He blew dust off the top of a box, sending it flying into the air in a cloud. "As you can tell, I never come up here."

Since I found Poppy Rose, the reporters had unearthed the story Regina had told me. In almost every newspaper, Poppy Rose was portrayed as a child arsonist who had murdered her entire family. There were pictures of Poppy Rose to accompany the stories now. Her bright eyes were large and unassuming as they called her a murderer. I hated those stories. I defended her against the locusts on every online paper. I hated what they did to her, what they made her out to be. She had been only a little girl at the time of the fire and now she was dead.

More than ever, I felt attached to her. Her family was all dead now too, I was the one left to protect her. I hoped something of her survived.

"Where should we start?' Harry asked.

"I think we should get a dumpster. Most of the stuff is going to be trash. With the smoke damage we won't be able to donate it, but we still need to go through everything. We don't want to throw out something important."

My eyes fell on a box labeled 'pictures'. I opened it. The photograph on top was the same one Regina had shown me of

Poppy Rose and her brothers at her house. I wondered if it was in fact the one I had seen. The brass frame looked really familiar. I brought it up to my nose to smell it for smoke. "What happened to the things from Regina's Cape May home?" I asked.

"You're looking at it," Harry said, taking the photo from me. "She had so much stuff, I just kinda put it anywhere I found space. So unfortunately her things are now mixed in with the stuff from Hoffman House."

I was right, this *was* the picture Regina had shown me. "That's Poppy Rose," I said, pointing to her in the photograph, unsure if Harry knew what she looked like. "And her brothers Peter and Patrick. The dark-haired boy is the gardener's son."

"Yeah, that's my dad," he said, handing me back the framed photograph.

My eyes widened. "I can't believe I didn't put that together when I met you. What's your dad's name?"

"Derrick."

"That's right, Derrick! Wow, I didn't realize your dad knew Poppy Rose."

"The whole family. He was very close with them."

"They look like they all could be brothers. Don't they? Even with your dad's dark gray eyes and brown hair."

"There was a rumor that he was."

"That your dad was a Hoffman?" I asked, examining the picture.

"My grandmother had been with my grandfather for years without children. So, when my father came along there were some rumors about how that came to be."

"Did you ever submit for a DNA test? Did Regina know?"

"She knew of the rumors, I'm sure of that. But she never took any stock in them."

"Why?"

"It's true my father looked like the Hoffman brothers and Poppy Rose too, but that's because their mother and my father's mother were sisters. That's how the Hoffmans first got incorporated into the family business. My grandfather gave his brother-in-law a job."

"That makes a lot of sense. It's why Mr. Hoffman let the Greenes stay on the estate. They were family," I said, my mind wheeling. "But wait! I don't get it. Regina left me the house because she had no family. But you *are* family. Even if you're not a Hoffman, you're Poppy Rose's cousin."

"It's true we're cousins, but it doesn't matter." He picked up a stack of photos from the box and thumbed through them. "It wouldn't have mattered to her if I took a DNA test and it came back confirming I was a Hoffman. Let's just say Regina didn't like my father very much."

My eyes narrowed. "Why was that?"

"He wasn't as loyal to the Hoffmans as I am."

"But you're not your father. Why not leave you everything?"

He shrugged. "It's like I told you when we met, I thought I *was* going to inherit everything, but I have always trusted Regina's judgement. It's like you said, she took care of me. She brought us together, and that's way better than a hunk of land."

"Harry and Juliet," I said, overjoyed.

He wrapped me in his arms. "Harry and Juliet forever."

I couldn't help myself; I'm such a mood killer. "Did your father ever talk about Poppy Rose going missing?"

"Yeah."

"What did he say?" I asked in a leading way.

Harry exhaled loudly through his nose as he released me from his hug. "You're not going to want to hear it."

"Now you have to tell me!"

"Only if you promise to put this off until we get a dumpster," he said, scanning the boxes.

"Deal."

He leaned on a stack of dusty boxes, releasing another surge of dust into the air. I swallowed my sneeze. "My father said she did it. Said Poppy Rose started the fire. He tried to stop her, but it was too late. The fire was lit, and she ran off. He tried to warn the Hoffmans, but Poppy Rose had started the fire in the hall that led to the bedrooms. They died, all of them, from smoke inhalation."

I felt sick to my stomach, a knot twisting deep inside of me. "Was he telling the truth?" I asked.

"He believes it. My father was key in identifying Poppy Rose as a suspect in the fire."

"That's why Regina didn't like your dad and why she didn't leave you the property in her will. He started the witch hunt."

He nodded. "She hated him. It wasn't until after Stephanie died that they came to some sort of friendly terms."

"It could have been your father who started the fire and blamed Poppy," I blurted out, wishing I hadn't just said that. This was Harry's father I was talking about; but I had looked into Poppy Rose's eyes—granted, via a photograph—and found her innocent. I needed to meet Harry's father. Then I would know for sure.

Harry shrugged, seemingly not bothered that I had just called his father a potential murderer. Relief washed over me. I thought we were about to have our first fight. "He could have, that's possible," Harry admitted. "It was his word the fire chief went on. Poppy wasn't there to defend herself."

"What about Match?" I asked.

"What about him?" Harry said, his posture stiffening. It was only slightly, but I still noticed it.

"Well, for starters, Match is holding a match, and fires are generally started with matches," I pointed out as kindly as I could. The sage I burned all day and night had seemed to work. I hadn't glimpsed the ghost boy, but that didn't mean I had forgotten about him.

"It wasn't him."

I raised an inquisitive brow. "You sure?"

"Yeah, I'm sure. Match is my friend. He wouldn't hurt anyone."

CHAPTER NINE
A Twist of Fate

Armed with a hand full of trash bags, I went upstairs. Romeo was by my side. His winter coat was already coming in, which meant he was tracking more cat litter around the house than ever. It was like he was rolling around in the stuff.

I had changed Romeo's litter to an organic brand, but it didn't help. Romeo left his little pawprints everywhere. I didn't mind; I loved him, and I loved Harry.

Summer was over and the leaves were turning autumnal hues. Things were still perfect with Harry. The honeymoon period never wore off, and I didn't think it ever would. I had never been happier.

I quit my job and found one closer to Greene Mills. It wasn't the best gig. I was still getting spit on every day (hazards of the profession) but it was an improvement.

My lease with Rick was officially over and it had been months since I heard from him. He had called me right after Harry helped me move out. He was ranting that I took the TV I gave him for Christmas and wanted it back. It was true, I took his TV, and admittedly, I was a little bit of a witch for doing that, but he shouldn't have pushed me.

Harry had overheard me talking to Rick and got on the

phone. He told him in this creepy voice, "You were warned." It must have scared the shit out of Rick because he didn't call again. And that was that.

Cleaning out the upstairs proved to be a slow process. After I found out the cost of a dumpster, we decided to forgo it. I didn't want to risk asking Mr. Davison for money for the dumpster. I was worried if I went that route, he would tell me I couldn't throw the stuff upstairs out. So, trash bag by trash bag, we cleared out the upstairs. I was off every Friday and dedicated Friday mornings to the cause.

I had just cleared away a stack of boxes and was about to call it quits for the day and make lunch, when I noticed a box labeled 'PR'.

I rushed to open it, hoping 'PR' stood for Poppy Rose. I hadn't found anything that had belonged to her and feared her things were lost to the fire that had claimed the lives of her two brothers and father.

If I was being honest with myself, the hope of finding something that belonged to her was the thing that kept me coming up there every Friday morning. I had gotten used to Harry's man cave setup and found it cozy. Sure, we could use more space (who couldn't) but we didn't need it.

I had felt a strong connection to Poppy Rose from the beginning, and that feeling only grew. Even after she stopped making the headlines, she was on my mind. I thought about her all the time—wondered if it was really possible that she started the fire, wondered how she came to be in my parents' backyard.

Harry was very anti-me meeting his dad, which was frustrating. I knew it was hard for him to talk about his father without thinking of his sister, so I didn't push him on the subject. I knew eventually I would meet him and when I did, I would ask him about the night of the fire.

Opening the cardboard box labeled 'PR', I found a stuffed dog. It smelled horribly of smoke. It stank worse than anything else I had found so far. I tossed it in a trash bag; there was no saving it. From the box, I pulled out a china doll. The doll had been glued back together, leaving its face marred with cracks and fissures. There were more stuffed animals and a few books. What drew my attention was a journal. It was locked. There wasn't a key at the bottom of the box, but that wasn't going to stop me. After finding the doll, I was sure the journal belonged to Poppy Rose.

I picked up Romeo, who was lounging in a box, and headed downstairs with him and the journal.

Breaking into the journal was harder than I thought possible, but with a little elbow grease and a box cutter, I was able to cut the binding off.

I took a seat at the kitchen table and opened it to read: Property of Poppy Rose Hoffman. A nervous energy pervaded my fingertips as I picked up the photograph that was placed in the front of the journal. It was summer and a young Regina—well, a younger Regina—was sitting on a blanket in the grass. Poppy Rose sat next to her on one side, and on the other sat a boy with large dark eyes and dark hair. Poppy Rose's brothers and Derrick Greene could be seen running around behind them.

My attention was brought back to the boy sitting next to Regina. He bore a strong resemblance to her. They both had large eyes and a beaked nose. The boy, in particular, looked like his eyes were too large for his face. I recognized those eyes. It was Match, Harry's ghost friend. I couldn't wait to show him. I turned the photograph over, hoping for a name, but there was none.

Tucking the photo back into the journal, I eagerly read:

Dear Journal,

I wish they would leave him alone. I don't know why they have to be so mean to him. They know he's our brother, but they insist on treating him that way. I know Peter and Pat think they are funny, but they aren't. It makes Derrick sad. Derrick wants to live in the big house with us, but he can't because of Mr. Greene. Daddy said it would kill him like it killed Momma if he knew the truth.

Dear Journal,

Derrick is getting mean—mean like my brothers and my dad. I don't want him to change. Me, him, and Eugene are best friends. But today he broke Dolly to make Peter and Pat laugh. He said he was sorry and helped me glue her together, but it was too late. Dolly will never be the same and I think the same goes for Derrick. It's like something has gotten into him. He's so different now. It's like he's not my brother anymore, but someone else. Not even Peter or Pat ever broke Dolly. I'm worried about Derrick and so is Eugene.

Dear Journal,

Derrick did a bad, bad thing. He hurt Eugene really bad. I'm so scared he's going to hurt me to keep me quiet. I promised I wouldn't tell anyone, but I don't think he believes me.
Poor Eugene. We all knew he was scared of the dark. He screamed and he screamed when Derrick put him in the salt shed. I tried to stop him, but he pushed me. Peter and Pat were no help. They thought it was funny Eugene was crying. They made fun of

him, teasing him and calling him names. I'm scared of the dark too, but they said that was normal because I'm a girl. They told Eugene he had to grow up.

I went to get Mr. Greene, but Derrick yanked my arm back, throwing me to the ground. Derrick used to love Eugene but now he hates him. I think it's because Mr. Greene likes Eugene the best. I think that's because he knows Eugene is his real son. But that's not Eugene's fault.

Derrick looked down at me with eyes so large and dark I didn't think they were his and told me, "Keep your mouth shut Poppy or I'll put you in the dark too, and I won't give you a match."

I was too scared to do anything. I just watched as Derrick tore a match from a match book and threw it at Eugene where he was shaking in the salt shed. Eugene scrambled to pick it up. He held the match to his chest as if it would protect him from the dark, but it was unlit.

I've always been scared of the salt shed. It's dark and it smells of dirt. It's darker there than it is at night. At night there is the moon and little stars. In the salt shed there is nothing.

Eugene sobbed as he begged his brother not to lock him in there. Derrick didn't care. He did it with a smile on his face. He shut the door and locked it. Eugene screamed and screamed. It was so loud I covered my ears, but then, all of a sudden, the screaming stopped.

"Let him out," I yelled, grabbing the keys to the salt shed from Derrick and yanking open the door. Eugene was on the ground. Blood was dripping from his nose. His eyes were rolled back in his head. I could only see white. As if his body was made of electricity, it twitched. Derrick wouldn't let us get Mr. Greene. He said we would all be in trouble if we did. Instead, they buried him.

* * *

I was shaken, my body physically trembling by the time I was done reading Poppy Rose's last journal entry. Eugene Greene had suffered a seizure, and they buried him alive. I didn't want to believe what I read, but I did. I felt it. I knew it was the truth. Match was Derrick's brother. Or at least they grew up as brothers. Derrick Greene was a Hoffman, Poppy Rose confirmed it. Everyone in the family seemed to know besides the Greenes, but Poppy Rose hinted that maybe Mr. Greene *did* know the truth.

I assumed Derrick being the son of Mr. and Mrs. Greene was the front that kept their marriage together. But Eugene, was he the product of their marriage or was he like Derrick, the result of infidelity? I thought Eugene looked too much like Regina to believe he was anything but her son. I couldn't have been the only one who saw the resemblance. That would have been one heck of a scandal at the time, as Regina never married. It made sense that Eugene was raised as a Greene. It protected the family.

If Poppy Rose broke her vow of silence and told Regina what happened to Eugene, it would reinforce why she hated Derrick. Eugene was dead and it was Derrick's fault.

Going to the kitchen sink, I splashed cold water on my face. I needed that. I could also use a tall glass of wine, but settled for a glass of water.

Turning around, I saw Match standing next to the kitchen table. My pulse soared, my heart beat in my ears as if my brain and heart had swapped places. I hadn't seen Match since that first night. The sage had worked at keeping him away, or didn't it?

Not wanting to risk looking at the incense burner and have Match disappear, I kept my eyes glued to him. I could still smell the earthy aroma of the sage and knew the burner didn't go out.

The sage didn't work, and I wondered if Harry knew that and let me burn it for a false sense of security, a security I could never get back now. Harry had said Match was harmless and rarely showed, but twice was too much for me, even knowing what had befallen him. I didn't trust his dead eyes. They were darker in the daylight and his complexion was paler, a strange milky hue. There was something not right about that. It should have been the other way around. Recognizing this, the little hairs on my arms bristled one at a time, until they all stood on end.

Like the first time I saw him, Match held a lit match in one hand while he shielded it with his other, as if a vagrant wind could come and snuff it out at any moment.

"I know who you are," I said in a whisper. "You're Eugene Greene. You're Harry's Uncle."

His dull, dark eyes glanced down at the journal on the table before returning to me.

"Yes," I said, keeping my voice low. "I read it in Poppy Rose's journal. Derrick wasn't your real brother, but your cousin, and he tortured you and buried you alive."

He shook his head before he lowered his hand to the journal. The pages lit immediately as if they had been doused in gasoline. In an instant, an orange fireball swallowed the journal.

At the sight of the fire, my breath caught. A hundred questions were racing through my head. Match stood there and watched the journal burn and as he did his pupils dilated until all that was left was darkness. He glanced at me, his black eyes holding me in a vacant stare. He shook his head at me again, this time methodically, right left, right left, before he vanished.

I raced to the kitchen table and threw my glass of water on the journal. It wasn't enough. I grabbed the pitcher of water from the refrigerator and dumped it over the crackling flames. That did the trick. The fire was out, the journal smoldering. The pages were black crisps. The photo of Regina and Eugene was lost forever. The house reeked of smoke, and I couldn't help but think this is what the Hoffmans smelled right before they died.

CHAPTER TEN
Derrick Greene

I finally understood why Harry was opposed to me meeting his father. It wasn't necessarily because they had bad blood between them, but because Derrick Greene was in a long-term care facility.

After he lost his daughter, he had a nervous breakdown. Harry told me that shortly after Stephie passed, his mother committed suicide and that's when his father went to Helping Hands Home. Harry stayed with Regina until he was sixteen and was legally emancipated. At that point, she gave him a place to live and a job.

Harry saw his father once a month, and warned me he got agitated very easily, resulting in his visits being cut short.

I didn't tell Harry about Poppy Rose's journal or Match burning it. He seemed to be very protective of Match. I could understand why. Harry's childhood was turbulent, and Match was his best friend—his so-called conscience. He trusted him. He had saved him from sharing the same fate as his sister. I didn't want to draw a line between trusting Match or trusting me.

After reading Poppy Rose's journal and the fire show on the kitchen table, it would be easy to assume Match lit the fire that killed the Hoffman family for revenge. Yet Harry's father had told him Poppy Rose did it.

I hadn't mentioned Eugene or asked Harry about his uncle. Harry hadn't mentioned having one, but that didn't mean he didn't know he existed. I wanted to talk with Derrick before I said anything. I was treading on a tender subject. Dropping the bomb that his father murdered his uncle before I got the facts straight could be the start of the end of us.

There were a lot of unknowns. I couldn't take everything Poppy Rose wrote in her journal at face value. She was just a little girl when she penned those pages. I just hoped Derrick Greene wasn't too far gone.

After we checked in at the visitor's desk, Harry and I were escorted to a large room that had many tables and chairs. Immediately, I was able to pick out Derrick Greene amongst the other patients. Harry looked like his father. They had the same brown hair and steel eyes.

"Hi Dad," Harry said, taking a seat across from his father. "I want you to meet my girlfriend, Juliet Winslow." I took a seat next to Harry. His father stared off into space as if he didn't hear him. "She wanted to meet you," Harry told him, taking my hand and squeezing it. "Things are getting serious between us, and I thought she was right, that it was time she met you. She has to know what she's getting into, in any case."

Harry was right about things getting serious. In the last week, we'd talked about marriage twice and even googled cool kid's names. I wanted to marry Harry, and I wanted kids. Maybe not a school bus full of screaming babies like Harry wanted, but a few. I told him, before all that could happen, I had to meet his father. He had met my parents on several occasions; it was only fair.

Derrick Greene's eyes slowly found his son's. "Then you told her about Stephanie?"

"I have."

"And about the others?" Derrick asked, quirking an eyebrow in my direction. He looked every bit as insane as I knew he must be.

"Dad," Harry said in a stern voice. "I want this to be a pleasant visit. That is, if you want Juliet and me to come back."

Derrick's eyes locked on to mine. I fought back a shudder. He had a harshness to his mouth that made me think of Rick. I knew then that Derrick was a cruel man, just as Poppy Rose's journal had made him out to be. He looked exactly like the kind of man who would lock his brother in the dark, knowing he was petrified of it.

I faked a series of coughs. "Harry, honey, can you get me a cup of water please?"

"Of course," he said, getting up.

As soon as Harry was out of earshot I said, "I know about Eugene. I know you locked him in the salt shed, and that you buried him alive."

Derrick scrunched his eyebrows, a deep furrow forming between them.

"That's right, I know. I found Poppy Rose's journal," I told him, not wanting to waste time playing games. "What I want to know is why did you warn Harry not to go to the Hoffman House, and what really happened to Poppy Rose?" I made sure not to mention the fire. I didn't want to put the thought in his brain.

"You don't understand," he muttered, shaking his head. "All I ever tried to do was protect them."

"Who, the Hoffmans?" I asked in a rushed voice, glancing across the room at Harry. I didn't have much time.

"Everyone. Eugene was infected. He wasn't my brother anymore. Poppy Rose couldn't see past the mask he wore. Peter or Patrick either, but they helped anyway. You have to understand,

Eugene wasn't Eugene when I put him in the salt shed. That's what I was trying to prove to them."

"But you buried him."

"I had to, while he was weak, before I couldn't contain him. We buried him in the basement of the house."

"Of the gardener's cottage?"

"Hoffman House. No one would look for him there. I didn't know it at the time, but when Poppy went to Eugene after he collapsed in the salt shed, the darkness got into her."

"Darkness?" I asked, thinking of Eugene's soulless eyes. I could feel the blood under my skin. I felt itchy.

"That's what I call it, the darkness. The darkness seeks light. Darkness always seeks out the light . . . and snuffs it out."

Harry returned, handing me a cup of water in one of those flimsy paper cups you always find at the dentist. "Thank you," I said before taking a sip.

"Harry," Derrick cooed, his voice taking on a sickly-sweet tone. "Be a good boy and get Juliet and me some cookies from the kitchen. I'm allowed cookies when I have a visitor."

"You okay?" Harry asked me, his hand running over the small of my back. It was little gestures like this from Harry that made my heart smile. He never missed the opportunity to let me know he cared. Actions speak louder than words, and his always did.

"Yeah, I'm fine. Cookies sound good."

I waited for Harry to leave through the double doors before I asked, "So, what happened with Poppy Rose?"

"Poppy Rose was convinced she had to kill her family for Eugene. Not for revenge, if that's what you're thinking, but because Eugene didn't want to be alone. You see, the same sickness that had been in him was now in her, and it wanted light. It wanted lives. She started the fire at the house, and I chased her. She didn't get far. I knew where she was going. She could only go to one place and that was Regina's. When I caught up with her, I snapped her neck. She was such a little thing; she broke so easily in my hands." He glanced down at his hands in his lap. "I'm still surprised by it, by how easy it was."

Impulsively, I covered my mouth with my palm. Poppy Rose hadn't died of exposure, she was murdered. When I scooped her skull from its resting place, I had inadvertently obscured the fact that her neck had been broken.

"It wasn't Poppy Rose I killed, Juliet. I loved Pesky Poppy Rose; that's what I always called her: Pesky Poppy Rose. She was my sister. She was my best friend. The darkness killed her long before I did." He sighed, his entire body decompressing before he continued. "I hid her body in the salt shed in a bag of salt until I was able to get rid of it. The next landscaping job I helped my father with, I disposed of her corpse in the woods."

I wiped my hot tears with my thumbs, careful not to smudge my make up. Poppy Rose came to rest in my parents' backyard at random, but I couldn't truly accept that. It was fate's design. I was meant to find her.

Derrik leaned in, dropping his voice to a near whisper. "Juliet, you can think what you want of me but listen to me very carefully. I am *not* crazy. I committed myself because the darkness got into me too, and I didn't want to kill for it. Harry is not who you think he is. He has the same sickness, the same one Eugene and Poppy Rose had. He got it when he went into Hoffman House. He infected the entire family. I told him not to go there but he did anyway, and he brought it home with him."

I felt rigid as if my blood went cold. "What are you saying?"

"You're not the first girl Harry has brought to see me and you won't be the last. He can't hide behind his good looks forever.

His mask starts to crack. Let me help you crack it, Juliet. Visit the salt shed. It's near the family cemetery."

I could feel my face twist in confusion. "I had no idea there was a cemetery on the property."

"No, you wouldn't. Harry doesn't want you to know what he's up to. You'll find what you're looking for where the Greene side of the property butts up against the Hoffman side and the woods."

Harry came back and placed vanilla cookies with red icing on a napkin in front of his father and me. As Harry pressed a chaste kiss to the side of my face, Derrick took a bite of a cookie and smiled. His teeth were painted red, and it reminded me of blood.

CHAPTER ELEVEN
A Date with Destiny

With the days getting shorter and the nights getting longer, it was late morning before Harry left for work the next day. As soon as his truck was out of sight, I zipped up my coat and headed in the direction of the salt shed. When I'd first read about it in Poppy Rose's journal, I was unsure if it was on the property but decided to do a quick walk through of Harry's greenhouse and the other sheds that were near the cottage in search of it. In truth, I wasn't sure if one of the buildings I had seen was the salt shed or not. After visiting Harry's father, I knew I hadn't found it. There wasn't a cemetery to mark it as the *salt shed.* Thirty acres is a lot of land, so I wasn't surprised I hadn't run across the family burial ground, but it was one of those kinds of oddities you would think your boyfriend, soon to be fiancée, would have mentioned.

A mix of emotions ran through me as I walked the property line, the grass on the Greene side of the property bleak in comparison to the lush emerald lawn of the Hoffman side. Part of me felt like, by buying into Derrick's craziness, I was betraying Harry. I loved Harry. I trusted Harry. He was perfect . . . maybe *too* perfect. Maybe that was why I hadn't told him what his father said. Maybe within Derrick's wild story, there were pockets of truth.

I shook my head at myself. I was being ridiculous. Harry's father was mentally unstable. He was where he was for a reason, but he'd warned me with such conviction, such unwavering certainty, I'd be amiss not to check. What I was checking on or for, I had no idea. Derrick made it seem like Harry was storing dead bodies in the salt shed, just like he had done with Poppy Rose's corpse. I wasn't a psychiatrist or anything, but I thought there was a pretty good chance Derrick was self-projecting—playing out the past in his head and replacing himself with a younger version of him in Harry.

I would go to the salt shed and then I would let the whole business with Eugene and Poppy Rose rest. Maybe that was what Match was trying to tell me by burning Poppy's journal—let it go. Harry seemed to think he steered him out of trouble, acting as his conscience, maybe the same went for me. That would have been easier to believe if he didn't have those eyes.

After miles of walking, I finally made it to the edge of the property. Sure enough, butting against a hill was a small cemetery, just like Derrick had described. There were about two dozen small headstones that jutted from the grass in neat rows. Cutting through the center of the gravestones was a gravel path that led to a building that was part of the hill. It reminded me of *Bilbo Baggins's* house, but in place of the cute round door that you would expect to see in a hobbit's home, there was a large iron one. The door stood slightly ajar and was coated in a layer of flaking orange rust. I knew what I was looking at was indeed the salt shed. I stared at the eroding door, at the sliver of darkness visible, unsure if I should enter or turn back. It wasn't too late to turn back.

The delicate little hairs on the nape of my neck stood at attention as a gust of wind whipped around the cemetery in a howl, leaving me covered in gooseflesh. Everything in me told me not to enter the salt shed—screamed at me to head back to the gardener's cottage and drop it. But that meant I *had* to go in. If there really was some strange sickness that affected Harry, and he was in trouble, I needed to know what I was up against—that is, if I was going to help him. Or it could just be a creepy shed built into a hill in the middle of a graveyard that a crazy man sent me to, and I was overreacting. But then again, I hadn't been able to shake the image of Match's eyes from my head. Those strange dull eyes that were nothing but darkness.

Using my phone's flashlight, I slowly took the salt shed's steps one at a time, descending into shadows. The salt shed was more like a salt cellar. It was cold and dank and full of salt; the smell of mold and moisture was prevalent. Salt and snow shovels and chains for tires, and typical landscaper tools to combat snowy weather. One of the bags of salt had torn open. Salt was sprinkled over the dirt floor like snow. I realized this must be what Romeo was trekking around the house. It was salt, not litter, that left his little pawprints everywhere.

"Just a crazy old man," I muttered to myself in relief as I headed up the stairs. I felt instantly better being out of the dark salt shed and in the fresh air.

I had just started down the path that cut through the cemetery when I stopped dead in my tracks. On the back of the headstones, I noticed names had been hand carved in them. It was crudely done, like the names I had seen on the flagstones that marked the foundation to the old Hoffman House.

I couldn't imagine kids coming all the way out here to deface an old cemetery, but what else could explain it? I searched the headstones for other signs of vandalism.

My heart felt like it exploded when my eyes landed on the name Paris France carved into the back of a headstone. The physical assault continued, my stomach clinching, almost making me double over as I read Margaret May's name. She was Harry's only girlfriend besides me who had the privilege of being spooked by Match. I found Judy Garwood's name quickly. Her name was carved into the back of the headstone next to Margaret May's. The crudely etched names were all women's names. I could only assume that they, at one time, had all been Harry's girlfriends.

"No, no, no, no, this can't be right," I said to myself. Or could it? This was what Derrick had alluded to. "NO!" I said again, with such force that it winded me. "Harry wouldn't hurt anyone."

My mind went to Rick and how Harry had threatened to make him disappear. "Oh God, Rick," I muttered, dialing him. I hadn't heard from Rick since Harry got on the phone with him, and I feared there was a reason why.

The call went to voicemail. "Rick, it's Juliet. I want to return your TV. Call me as soon as you get this."

If Rick was alive, he would call me back. He loved that TV more than he ever loved me.

My phone rang, it was Rick. "Rick!"

"Yeah, it's me."

"Thank goodness," I said, my voice cracking. "I need your help. That guy I'm dating, he's a serial killer! I don't know what to do."

"Where are you at now?"

"His place, at the salt shed."

"Don't do anything. Stay put, I'm close. I'll be right there."

The phone clicked off and my heart pounded faster in my chest. I couldn't think. All I could hear was it thrashing about. Romeo appeared from behind a headstone and trotted up to me. I picked him up and buried my face in his soft fur. It was nice to have someone to hold.

At the sound of footfalls, my head snapped up. Harry was

coming my way. Panic coursed through my veins. If I made a run for it, he'd catch me. There was no doubt in my mind he would catch me. My best bet was to play it off and act like I saw nothing.

"Hey Juliet, what are you doing all the way back here?" Harry asked.

I held Romeo out for Harry to see. "Chasing Romeo," I lied. "He's due for his flea medicine and the little bugger ran out the cat door. I didn't want to waste the tube, those things are soooo darn expensive, so I followed him out here. Now that the little gray dust ball has been caught, it's time to go back in the house for his flea medicine and a treat."

"Hey," I heard from behind me. It was Rick, he was jogging our way. I released Romeo and ran into Rick's arms. He squeezed me and as he did, I realized something terrifying. I never told Rick where Harry lived. And on top of that, how did he get there so quickly? I let go of Rick to see a smug grin plastered on his face.

Rick glanced Harry's way. "I told you big bro, you can't trust this one. I'd know," he said, grabbing himself in a crude gesture. "But hey, you're the one who wanted my sloppy seconds."

"Big bro?" I contemplated, my eyes darting to Harry.

Harry nodded. "I was as surprised as you are when I showed up at your place and the jerk that pushed you was my own kid brother. I didn't say anything, because I was afraid if I did, you wouldn't give us a chance. I'm nothing like Rick."

Thinking back, Rick did call Harry *broski*, but I thought nothing of it. He called everyone that. I knew Rick had a brother and father he didn't talk to, but Harry had only mentioned his sister and now I knew why.

"Come on bro, that's not true, we're both killers," Rick said, before locking eyes with me. "Didn't you know that, Jules? We're both bona fide killers. And I'm going to have so much fun watching you die. You never mess with a man and his television. You're gonna learn that lesson the hard way, you little bitch."

Harry pointed at his brother and said in the same creepy tone he'd used with him before, "Touch her and I'll kill you."

"Come off it already, *Harold*. You gave it a try and she doesn't trust you. If she did, we wouldn't be here right now."

On his phone, Rick played back our conversation for Harry. "Thank goodness. I need your help. That guy I'm dating, he's a serial killer! I don't know what to do."

"Harry," I said, distancing myself from Rick the Dick. "I saw the names on the tombstones. What was I supposed to think?!"

"You weren't out here because of Romeo. My father sent you here, didn't he?" Harry asked with glazed eyes.

I nodded.

"Oh Juliet, if only you'd trusted me, we could have avoided all of this," Harry said, pushing his hair off his forehead. "I'm not a bad guy. I swear. You just don't understand."

"Make her understand," Rick said mockingly.

"You know when I said the grounds were sick?" Harry asked me, his voice pleading.

"Yes," I said, doing my best to keep myself together.

"I'm trying to make it better. You see, Match was my father's younger brother Eugene, and he was murdered by my father when he was a boy. He was buried in the land and after that the land got sick. Eugene was terrified of the dark and he died terrified. He didn't pass on, he couldn't. He's in the cold, dark ground. He doesn't want to be alone. He's scared and he needs people with him."

My body trembled, my knees knocking together. That was almost exactly what Derrick had told me.

"It's not what you're thinking, Juliet," Harry said, blinking back tears. "We don't kill for him. My father thinks we do, but that's just not true. We're helping the family, just like Poppy Rose."

"What are you talking about?" I asked, taking a deep breath to steady my nerves.

"Poppy Rose started that fire to save her family," Harry told me. "The Hoffman's had just gotten back from a vacation that had left everyone in the family besides Poppy Rose deadly ill. The family physician diagnosed it as Dengue fever and called an ambulance. They were beyond help and would have died in the hospital. They had to die on Hoffman property and had to be buried with Match, if they were to come back. Poppy Rose started the fire right after the doctor left. Her father and brothers were too weak to leave their beds and died. But they didn't die Juliet, not in the way you're thinking. Can't you see them? They're all around us."

I spun around, hoping to glimpse Match, hoping to glimpse anyone. I didn't want to believe Derrick Greene. I saw nothing. There was nothing besides grass and trees. "I don't see them, Harry," I said, my voice trembling.

"I had high hopes you would. When you saw Match right away, I thought it was a sign you and I were meant to be together. Match thought it too."

I realized then that I'd been right—Match had wanted me to let it go. He burnt the journal so I wouldn't go see Derrick and end up right where I was. He had tried to save me.

"The same went for Stephie," Harry told me, his eyes sheets of tears. "She was terminally ill. She had leukemia. The doctors gave her two weeks to live." I thought of Stephie's room and the wigs. They were for more than just playing dress up. Cancer had claimed her hair. "My father forbid Ricky and me from taking her to the house. But we didn't listen, did we?" Harry posed, glancing to his brother.

"No. We took her to Hoffman House, and we helped her fall down the crumbling stairs," Rick said.

Hot tears rolled down my cheeks. I didn't know what to say or do. I felt like I was trapped in a nightmare.

"Don't cry, Juliet," Harry begged. "Stephanie's fine. She's not in pain, she's happy. She's with me right now. I wish you could see her, so you would know."

"She will, soon enough," Rick said. "Remember, Auntie R said if things went south with Juliet, she gets buried on the Hoffman side because of her connection to Poppy Rose."

"What are you talking about?" I asked, my eyes cutting to Rick.

"Dear old Dad didn't understand Poppy Rose was saving her family, not killing them," Rick told me. "When he chased Poppy down and killed her, she wasn't on Hoffman property and thus when we buried her remains at the site of the old Hoffman House, she didn't come back. Auntie R thinks there's a connection between you and Poppy Rose and hopes that through this connection Poppy Rose will be brought back along with you." Rick shrugged. "It's a long shot, but what Auntie R says goes."

There was no denying I felt a connection to Poppy Rose, but it wasn't like this Auntie R thought it was. There was nothing otherworldly about it. "Auntie R?" I asked.

"Regina," Harry answered in a soft voice. "Regina thought that fate had brought you to us and that we would be the start of a new generation of Hoffmans. It's why she left you the house. She wanted us to be together, but in the event she was wrong, she wanted you buried in the front yard with the family, just in case. She was overjoyed when you found Poppy Rose. My father couldn't remember where he had buried her. We had just about given up hope of ever recovering her remains, but then you came along Juliet and brought her home. We buried her remains within the flagstones, but like Rick said, she didn't come back. My father murdered her and there's nothing Match or any of us can do about it."

"And them?!" I said, pointing back at the headstones, my disbelief giving way to anger. "Did your father murder them too?!"

"They're false grave markers. All of the Hoffman's have been moved to the front yard under the green grass."

"I'm talking about Paris France and Margret May and all of the rest of them!"

"They're dead," Harry said flatly. "They're dead and they aren't coming back. They came here, each and every one of them after they met my father, and now they're dead and buried. I didn't want to hurt them but—"

"I did," Rick interrupted.

Harry tugged on his ear as a deep flush covered his cheeks and the bridge of his nose. "After they saw what they saw, I couldn't just let them leave. In the end, they gave me no choice. It was them or the family."

"And neither did you, Jules," Rick said, grabbing my arm. "Off to the front we go; you have a date with destiny."

I kicked at him but it was no use. Rick quickly overpowered me. He pulled a zip tie from his jacket pocket and zip tied my hands behind my back. The bastard was prepared.

He marched me to the front yard, the wind biting at my heels. Harry and Romeo followed behind us. As I crossed the sea of lush grass, I couldn't help but think about it being watered with my blood and how I would soon be the magic that made things pretty. That's how it went, after all. Why the Hoffman's had such a nice lawn, they had great fertilizer.

* * *

"Regina!" I said, not believing my eyes as Rick pushed me forward. "You're not dead!" Regina was sitting proudly in a wheelchair near the flagstone foundation of the old Hoffman House, very near to where I had sat, happy, a few months ago.

Sure, Rick and Harry had just mentioned her, but I hadn't imagined she was still alive; but it made sense. The lines in the grass I had noticed were from her wheelchair. Regina, unbeknownst to me, had been visiting the property. She had faked her own death and bequeathed me 74 Lockhart—all to get me to meet Harry so I could either pop out Hoffman babies, or she could bury me under the green grass in hopes that it would resurrect Poppy Rose's spirit. Fuck fate and fuck Regina. She had lied to me about everything, even about Poppy starting the fire that had killed her family. She had manipulated me. I was just a mark to her.

"Soon we will both be dead, my sweet Juliet," Regina told me in a calm voice. "But don't worry, we won't be dead for long. My nephews are going to bury us, just like my poor Eugene was buried, and together we will rise. I hope your connection to Poppy Rose will bring her home. I miss my little boy and her terribly."

"I don't want to die," I attempted to say firmly, but my voice came out feeble. My tears, on the other hand, flowed with the conviction I wished my words had.

Regina stood and made her way over to me while a smile teased her lips. She plucked a hair from my head. It looked reddish in the sunlight. With her fingers acting as a pair of scissors, she cut it in a similar gesture she'd made when I first met her for tea. "We all have to die," she said, sounding a lot like Rick. "But don't be scared Juliet. Death is only one adventure—more awaits for us."

I swallowed my tears. I wouldn't let one more fall. I refused to let the Hoffmans and the Fates get the best of me. Those three bitches could trip on their thread of life, hopefully with their scissors blade side-up. And the Hoffmans—they could all rot in the ground, even Harry.

My eyes darted to him. I didn't want Harry to rot any more than I wanted to die. I should want him dead, really dead and rotting. He, like Regina, had lied to me from the beginning. He had a secret double life as a midnight occult gardener. Trust the Greenes, my ass. He was a manipulator, a liar. He lied about Rick, lied about Regina, lied about the circumstances surrounding his sister's death, and so much more. He was *Pinocchio* with a dead boy as his conscience. I should want him double dead, but I didn't. I loved him. As crazy as it was, I loved him. Even knowing what he'd done, I still loved him.

The love I felt for Harry made me nauseous as the knot in my stomach tightened to a fist. I loved him and he was going to let me be buried alive. I couldn't believe he was going along with this. I know he didn't want to. His eyes were red-rimmed from crying; he couldn't hide that, no matter how good he was at wearing a mask. I heard him as he followed Rick and me. He tried to stifle himself, but I still heard.

As if Regina just read my mind, she told me in a reassuring tone, "Don't worry about Harry. He will find someone else."

"Someone more trustworthy," Rick snickered.

"Richard," Regina said in a stern voice, "stay out of this."

"I don't want to bury her," Harry told Regina softly. "I love her, Auntie R."

"He said that about all of them," Rick snorted.

I couldn't imagine what I ever saw in Rick. That's right—his height—his only good attribute. I really hated him. I wished I could cut him down to size.

"Please, Auntie R, she's the one. I know it. Match knows it too."

"Is he here?" Regina asked, tears welling in her eyes. "Is my little boy here?"

"He is," Harry confirmed. "He's next to me. He's shaking his head."

"Big whoop, he's shaking his head," Rick sneered. "Tell Match Boy to show himself to all of us. Tell him to fucking say something for a change. I don't like always having to take your word for it."

"You've never seen him, have you?" I asked Rick.

"Oh, and let me guess—you think you're special because you have?"

"I've seen him twice," I said. "So yeah, I feel pretty damn special. He must think so too, or maybe it's just that he thinks so little of you he doesn't bother to make an appearance when you're around."

"You're just saying that. You didn't see him twice," Rick said, frustrated. He glanced to Harry. "No one has seen Match more than once but Harry. You're just trying to save your skin, but it's not going to work." He pointed to a tarp on the ground. "Your final resting place is waiting for you, Jules."

I wished I would have told Harry I saw Match again. There was no way he would believe me now. Rick was right, it looked like I was using Match to try to save myself.

"You already dug the hole?" Harry asked as he removed the tarp.

I knew the answer to Harry's question before he asked it. There was a mountain of dirt next to the tarp. Rick had dug and dug until he had one hell of a deep hole. Seeing it—seeing the dark place that waited for me and smelling the rich earth that would become my eternal bed—spurred me into action. So much for dying with dignity.

I fought against Rick, who held my shoulders, to no avail. He dug his nails through my coat into my flesh, locking me in place. I glanced toward the street and wondered if the old woman was sitting on her rocking chair. I wondered if she could see me and if she could, if she would help. She'd warned me about the Hoffman boys, told me she saw blood on their hands, and I hadn't listened.

"Six feet deep, broski," Rick told Harry proudly. "When you told me you were taking her to see Dad, I knew what was coming next. I grabbed a shovel and called Auntie R. I finished this morning, just in time to take the call from Jules." He planted a wet kiss on the side of my face. "That's what I call kismet, baby."

"Harry," I pleaded in one last attempt to reach him, my dignity holding on by a thread. "Please, I love you. You know that. I really did see Match twice."

He bowed his head, his hair falling over his eyes. "Juliet, please don't make this hard on me."

"I am," I said, in the strongest voice I could muster. "I'm not going to make it easy on you. I'm going to make today the worst day of your life. I love you and you're going to put me in some hole like trash. What about our plans? What about our family? We were meant to be together—Harry and Juliet."

"Oh, please," Rick said, pushing me into the hole. "It's Romeo and Juliet, even I know that."

Landing on my side, I winced in pain.

"Hey, we should bury the cat with her, make it a real fairytale ending just like she always wanted," Rick laughed. He tossed Romeo into the hole and threw a scoopful of dirt over us. Romeo jumped out, clawing his way to safety. I did my best to wipe my face against my shoulder. Of course, Rick threw the shovel full of dirt on my face. I wouldn't expect anything less from him.

I stared up at Harry, who waited on the opposite side of the grave from where Rick was shoveling. There was no way I could get out of the hole with my hands tied behind my back, and where would I go if I could? I decided to just lay were I fell. This was really happening. Harry was going to let Rick bury me alive. Everything had brought me to this moment. I couldn't escape my fate. I was destined to find Poppy Rose. I was destined to meet Harry Greene, and I was destined to be buried alive by Rick the Dick.

I hoped being buried alive was like falling asleep on a bed of dirt. I had laid over Poppy Rose on her blanket of moss, and now I would serve as that bed to strangers, maybe even to Harry's next girlfriend. I wasn't a rabbit, and I wasn't *Alice*. I was Juliet, and my blood would paint the grass the brightest green anyone had ever seen.

Match appeared on his side next to me, breaking me out of my reverie, his face perfectly aligned with mine. His dark hair and clothing rippled around his marble face like murky water. His eyes were darker than pitch as they penetrated what felt like my soul. A shiver tiptoed down my spine, despite the abnormal warmth emanating from the match he held. Its blue flame shone brightly in the dark hole that was to serve as my final resting place. I knew only I could see him. If Harry or Rick did, or even Regina, someone would have said something, but no one said anything besides Match. He spoke to me in a whisper. "I am darkness, Juliet. Do you choose me and Harry or the worms?"

I knew he spoke the truth, I saw it in his eyes, it was just like Derrick said, he was darkness. "Harry. I choose Harry," I whispered back, my chest heaving as I was showered with more dirt. Match knelt over me. The heat from the match warmed my wrists as he put the flame to the zip tie. He disappeared as I pulled my hands apart. My hands free, I fought my way to my feet.

"Get down," Rick said, going to hit me with the shovel. I

grabbed it and pulled. Rick fell into the hole with me, landing on his back. Without hesitation, I put the shovel to his neck, fear evident in his dark eyes. My heart sounded like a war drum as I thrusted the shovel into his jugular. His warm blood sprayed all over me. It was in my eyes. In my mouth. The shovel was yanked from me. It was Harry. I put my hands up to brace myself for a blow and closed my eyes. I heard the ding of the shovel hitting the ground and felt his arms embrace me.

He hugged me to his chest. "I love you, Juliet. I love you so much."

"I killed Rick," I said, as if he didn't know. I kept my eyes closed as the shock of what I just did washed over me. "I killed him."

"He's not dead," Harry said to me in a kind voice.

I forced my eyes open and glanced over Harry's shoulder at Rick. He was dead, very dead. His eyes were wide open, frozen in shock, his own blood covering him in a blood mask. "He is," I sobbed, my tears streaming down my face.

He dried my tears with the sleeve of his jacket. "Not for long. Help me bury him."

"You're not going to kill me?" I asked, unsure, my voice wavering.

He pressed a kiss to my cheek. "I never wanted to, and now that you killed Rick, I don't have to. It's proof we're meant to be. You can't change your fate, Juliet. We were meant to be together and when we were about to be separated, fate stepped in. Things happened the way they were supposed to. You're one of us now. Harry and Juliet forever," he said, this time planting a kiss on my lips.

"Come on, let's bury Rick."

Harry climbed out of the hole and helped me up.

"Welcome to the family," Regina said, taking my hand and

squeezing it. "I knew when I met you, you would make my Harry happy."

"I am, Auntie R. We both are, aren't we, Juliet?"

I looked at Harry. Really looked at him. I loved him and he was right—I was one of them now. The sickness was in the Hoffman property, and in Harold Greene, and now it was in me. There was no turning back, I was a murderer. I had watered the grass with Rick's blood. Match intervened for fate and gave me a choice, and I chose Harold Greene. That meant I had to be okay with the occasional shovel to the throat in the name of the family. "Yes, Harry," I said, taking his hand. "I'm happy."

"Bury me with Ricky," Regina said. "I face death with a smile knowing I don't have to worry about my boys. At long last, it's time for me to be reunited with Eugene."

We helped Regina into the hole. She wrapped her arms around her nephew, and we covered them. It was dusk when we were done, but it wasn't dark out. The Hoffman grass was illuminated in pale figures.

I saw the Hoffman brothers, Peter and Patrick, and their parents. Rick was there too, in the grass. In place of his usual scowl was a smile. He was with his little sister, who had her arms wrapped around his waist. Her long blonde hair blew in the wind as if she never had cancer and never died. She was lovely and she was happy. My eyes traveled to Regina. She was young again and she was with Eugene as they had been in the picture I'd found in Poppy Rose's journal. Eugene no longer held a match, but his mother's hand.

There were many faces I recognized from the old photographs Harry and I found upstairs in the gardener's cottage, and many I didn't. I searched the pale faces for Poppy Rose, but she wasn't there. I wondered if she rested in peace, or if peace was what I was looking at.

Romeo brushed against my leg. I picked him up, holding him close to my chest. His soft purrs filled the night in a bittersweet song. Harry wrapped his arm around my shoulder, bringing our little family closer together. There was never any doubt in my mind that I was destined to find Poppy Rose, destined to meet Harold Greene, and destined to be happy. Thank you, Jack Cat.

The End . . .

THANKS FOR READING!

If this book helped you escape, if only for a moment, please consider taking the time to leave a review or star rating on Amazon or whatever platform you use. It would warm the cockles of my little, black heart to hear from you.

Looking for something else to read? Don't forget to check out my other books on Amazon.

Follow me on social media (I'm on all platforms under Holly Knightley). Sign up for my newsletter for the latest news, glimpse into my wacky process, and occasional freebie. Stay spooky and happy reading!

WANT MORE?